CW01329423

CURTAIN Call

ISRAEL BOOKSHOP
Publications

CURTAIN Call

M. JAKUBOWICZ

Copyright © 2016 by Israel Bookshop Publications

ISBN ISBN 978-1-60091-442-3

All rights reserved. No part of this book may be reproduced or transmitted in any form or by any means (electronic, photocopying, recording or otherwise) without prior permission of the publisher.

This book was originally serialized in the *Yated Ne'eman*.

Book design by Elisheva Appel

Distributed by:
Israel Bookshop Publications
501 Prospect Street / Lakewood, NJ 08701
Tel: (732) 901-3009 / Fax: (732) 901-4012
www.israelbookshoppublications.com / info@israelbookshoppublications.com

Printed in United States of America

Distributed in Israel by:
Shanky's
Petach Tikva 16
Jerusalem
972-2-538-6936

Distributed in Europe by:
Lehmanns
Unit E Viking Industrial Park
Rolling Mill Road,
Jarrow, Tyne & Wear NE32 3DP
44-191-430-0333

Distributed in Australia by:
Gold's Book and Gift Company
3- 13 William Street
Balaclava 3183
613-9527-8775

Distributed in South Africa by:
Kollel Bookshop
Northfield Centre
17 Northfield Avenue
Glenhazel 2192
27-11-440-6679

Dedicated in memory of my grandfathers

מרדכי בן צבי גרשון ע"ה

Who bought me my very first dictionary

and always inspired my love of the written word

with gentle encouragement and deep pride

and

יהודה אריה בן אהרן הלוי ע"ה

Whom I was never privileged to meet

but whose courage to rebuild after the flames of the Holocaust

serves as a legacy to his children and descendants

CHAPTER 1

Brachie

It's only Monday morning, and I'm dreading the rest of the day already.

I rub the sleep out of my eyes, trying to look awake and cheerful as Mrs. Bodner's daughter should look. I'm running late, which is already a strike against me. The Principal's Daughter should be a model of punctuality, should she not?

She should be a model of lots of other things, too…but I'm not even going there.

"Hi, Brachie," a voice calls from behind me.

The smile I paste on my chapped lips is born from years of habit.

"Good morning," I say pleasantly, before I even turn around to see who's there.

Atara Gold falls into step beside me, her purple knapsack dangling gracefully from her shoulder.

"It's cold today, isn't it?" she asks.

I nod, admiring her sparkling shoes stepping delicately beside my own sensible navy loafers. Atara is one of those girls who seem to have it all — grace, charm, and a father with a huge bank account.

"So…any idea what's happening during today's assembly?" Atara asks lightly.

I blanch, then immediately set my features in what I hope is a placid, poised expression. There it is — the real reason why Atara Gold is choosing to walk alongside Brachie Bodner, a.k.a. The Principal's Daughter.

Surely, she expects me to enlighten her as to the schedule for today's events. But I cannot — because I don't even know what they are myself!

I frown. What *would* my classmates say if they knew that The Principal's Daughter doesn't know all that much about top-secret events to which the principal is privy? That the close bond my mother advocates to adoring audiences does not personify our own relationship?

I swallow, hard, and turn my frown upside down, into the polite smile I use to mask my true feelings.

"I don't know," I say simply.

Is it my imagination, or is Atara's pace picking up as if she wants to get away from me faster and find her own tight-knit group of friends?

I tell myself that it doesn't matter. I remind myself that I don't care.

After all, I'm used to it.

Atara

MONDAY MORNING could not have started off on a worse foot.

I know that Mommy and Daddy are only away till the end of the week, but right now each day is looming ahead of me like a pitch-dark tunnel with no end in sight. As the oldest in my house, I know I have to pitch in. But it's kind of hard to do that when I oversleep by twenty-seven minutes.

"Atara!" my three little sisters call to me, frolicking around my bed like puppies at play. I smile as I sit up — but that smile fades when I see the thick blue numbers on my purple alarm clock.

"Help!" I screech as I jump out of bed.

Seven minutes later, I am pulling on my coat in our newly-decorated front hallway.

"Who's going to take us to school?" Esti asks anxiously.

"Who's going to give us our snack?" Elisheva wants to know.

"Who's going to pick us up from school?" Miri demands, tugging at my hand.

I gently extricate her hand from my own and look guiltily at my sisters. "Janet will take care of you," I say.

I can see our live-in hovering in the background, picking up the odds and ends my sisters have left lying around on the shining marble floor.

Esti pouts, and I fear a tantrum is brewing.

"Bye!" I say brightly, before pulling open the heavy front door and making my escape. I feel bad for these little girls who don't have parents for a full week. They will be shuffled from school to friends' houses, and then back to home for baths and a bedtime story — presided over by yours truly. Janet will remain a background figure, cleaning and making sure it all goes like clockwork. More than that, my mother would never allow. Her children are too precious to be left with nannies, she always says. So why did she have to go along on my father's business trip to Europe?

I inhale the frigid air, hardly aware of how the wind whips my face, and hurry along. I walk a few blocks, not really noticing how the majestic mansions turn into more modest two-story homes.

Then I see her.

A warm feeling fills my heart. I've always liked Brachie Bodner. She's such a nice, refined girl, and she really has her priorities straight. There's a constant smile on her face, her uniform is always neat and pressed, and she's kind to everyone.

Who doesn't like Brachie?

I greet her and make small talk about that day's assembly. I'm not so interested, truth be told, but it's something to shmooze about. So why does it seem like Brachie doesn't want to talk?

I sigh quietly. Sometimes I think that the only thing my classmates care about is what they can get from me. But I know Brachie isn't like that. With a mother like Mrs. Bodner, she's got to have grown up in the most amazing home ever. She has her *hashkafos* straighter than a pencil attached to a compass.

Maybe Brachie woke up on the wrong side of the bed?

Nah. Perfect girls like Brachie just don't do that. I peek at her and see that her trademark smile is stretched across her face.

I exhale in relief. So she's not upset or using me or anything like that.

I probably just imagined the whole thing.

Brachie

SOMETIMES my mother lets me in on behind-the-scenes secrets, but often I'm just as clueless as the other girls in my school. What she'd told me only the night before didn't really classify as a *secret*, but it wasn't exactly something I was going to share with my classmates.

I'll never forget how my oldest sister Dassi dealt with being our mother's daughter, back in the days when my mother was still a classroom teacher. Self-assured Dassi absolutely loved when my mother taught her class. If her classmates ever had a problem with any of my mother's policies, well, that was *their* problem.

But me…I lack the luster of Dassi's personality and the sparkle of her smiling eyes, the unique ability she has to laugh off whatever injustices come her way.

It's more than that, though. It's far more different for your mother to be your principal than it is for her to be your ninth-grade Chumash teacher.

I still don't understand why my older sisters — all four of them — thought I was so lucky when Ima was promoted. Had they any clue what it's like to have your classmates hash over the school's latest egregious policy, knowing full well that it was your mother who had spearheaded it? Did they have any idea what it's like for every single one of your teachers to know that your mother is their boss? Could they imagine what it's like for your classmates to tiptoe around you, ever wary that you'll carry some nefarious tidings right back to the principal?

No, they can't.

And I couldn't have imagined how hard it would be either, until I started high school.

My mother never fails to remind us that teaching in the classroom will always be her primary joy — and she takes any and all opportunities to do so. That's why, when Morah Beckerman called our house late last night saying she couldn't come in the next day, my mother assured her that no problem, she'd be happy to take over her classes.

Maybe my mother is happy about that. But I'm not.

If there's anything I like less than having my mother as the principal, it's having my mother as a teacher. So the expression "my heart fell" takes on new meaning this morning as I watch my mother step through the classroom door, to the confused murmurings of my classmates.

I gaze at the cracks in my desk as if they're the most fascinating things in the world. Anything to avoid the glances I know my classmates are casting my way. I'm sure they're wondering if I was in on this unexpected development. Well, I won't enlighten them. Let them wonder.

"Good morning, girls," my mother says, her tone simultaneously brisk and chirpy. Only my mother can pull that off. "Please take out your Chumashim."

I can tell my classmates are itching to ask where Morah Beckerman is and how long she's expected to be absent from school. But of course, they don't. Instead, they reach into their knapsacks and pull out notebooks and *sefarim*, as if it's perfectly normal for the principal to be standing in the front of our classroom, ready to begin teaching us.

My Chumash is already neatly settled in the corner of my desk, alongside my trusty notebook. I'm prepared, as usual, for that period's lesson.

"Baila, can you please read *perek beis, pasuk zayin*," my mother says. Her eyes glint, as they always do when she's about to jump headfirst into a lesson.

I heave a sigh of relief. I'm a good student, but it would be horrible if my mother singled me out to read the *pasuk*. I would be mortified, actually.

And that's why I'm caught off guard when I hear her say, "Very good, Baila. Brachie, can you please read the first Rashi and tell us what the question in the *pasuk* is?"

My face flames brighter than the fire engine I can hear zooming down the block. All I can think is, *Ima, how could you?*

I don't look up to meet my mother's glance, so I can't read the expression in her eyes or try to figure out what's going through her mind.

Instead, I slump a little lower in my seat and start to read the Rashi aloud.

Atara

AMAZING.

There's no other way to describe Mrs. Bodner's lessons. She doesn't teach us often, it's true, but every time she substitutes in our class, I feel more uplifted, more *real*, at the end of the period.

Mrs. Bodner is just one of those people who were born to teach. It's almost a shame that she's the principal.

I am thrilled when she walks into our classroom today, and I'm sure Brachie feels the same way. I wonder fleetingly if Mrs. Bodner is as much of a powerhouse at home as she is in school. Does she spout *hashkafah* as she peels potatoes? Lecture on the innate dignity of a Jewish princess as she sweeps the floor?

I wish I could get a glimpse into the Bodner home one day...

I think of my own empty house, with Janet at the helm this week. I blink quickly and look inside my Chumash.

Just then, I hear Mrs. Bodner pick Brachie to read, just as casually as she would pick anyone else in the class. I'm sure Brachie doesn't mind. Her mother called on her so naturally, so smoothly, it's easy to forget that Brachie is Mrs. Bodner's daughter. In fact, if it wasn't for the same regal bearing that characterizes both mother and daughter, I'd be inclined to not think about the relationship they share at all.

I am so swept up in the fast-paced lesson that the ringing of the bell almost comes as a surprise to me. I know that not all of my classmates appreciate a good lesson like I do, but I am taken aback when Rena Hoch, sitting in the back of the room, makes a snide comment about stolen free periods.

Some girls snicker, while others ignore her. I cannot help but remember a *pasuk* we learned last year: *Leitzanus achas docheh mei'ah tochachos*, that one line of mockery can destroy the accomplishments of a hundred lines of *mussar*. It's as if Mrs. Bodner's carefully-crafted lesson has been smashed to smithereens.

I would be mortified if I were her daughter.

I think of Brachie, and how only a girl like that can rise above these kinds of petty and rude comments. Only Brachie, I am sure, can remain unaffected by the insinuation that her mother "stole" our free time.

I wish I had just an ounce of her fortitude.

CHAPTER 2

Brachie

I AM MAD.

Burning mad, actually.

Rena Hoch has done it again. She's one of the only girls in my class who dares to comment on my mother in front of me — and she gets me every time. Of course, I'm good at pretending that I'm as thick-skinned as a rhinoceros. I wonder if it ever occurs to my classmates that the mud of Rena's barbs doesn't slide off my back as easily as I make it seem.

I stomp inside my house, hoping that my mother will be home and that she'll be available to talk to me. We don't do that so often. I can't help worrying that if I tell my mother too much, somehow it'll get back to my classmates. The last thing I want is to be known as an untrustworthy tattletale.

I hang up my coat and tuck my knapsack neatly into the corner of the foyer. I haven't needed a reminder to put away my things since…oh, I can't remember.

"Ima?" I call tentatively.

Suddenly, I hear an explosion of sound coming from the basement. I follow it down the stairs, wondering why I hear loud babbling and high-pitched giggles on a regular weeknight.

"Dassi!" I exclaim, catching sight of my oldest sister.

She's sitting on the ratty couch we keep in the basement — the one that came with our house when my parents bought it ages ago — with her black snood slightly askew. She smiles widely at me.

"Hi, Brachie! What's doing?"

"Baruch Hashem." I perch myself on the edge of the couch beside her. My mother is busy on the other side of the basement, clawing through several dark-green garbage bags.

"Hi, kids!" I say to my nieces and nephew. They're too busy frolicking around to even notice me.

"Hi, Brachie," my mother says, looking up for a moment. "How was your day?"

"Baruch Hashem," I reply, as I usually do. I'm relieved my perceptive mother is otherwise preoccupied, so she does not notice my lackluster tone.

"Great," my mother says, smiling. "Who likes this pretty sweater?" she asks, holding up a top I'd worn when I was little.

"Me!" Dassi's two little girls chorus.

"Me!" my tiny nephew joins in with an impish grin.

Even I laugh at his cute antics.

"This is only for girls," my mother tells Yechiel fondly.

Zissy and Tova prance around my mother, reaching for the sweater.

"I want it," Tova begs.

My mother holds it high and tosses it over to Dassi. "You decide who it fits," she says.

Dassi laughs, not at all perturbed when her girls race over to her, their springy dirty-blonde curls flying.

"It's *gemach* night," Dassi tells me, her eyes crinkling like she's telling a great joke.

"Oh?" I ask, raising my eyebrows.

"We're going through some old clothes Ima had hiding in the basement closet," Dassi explains.

I shrug. If Dassi doesn't mind our ancient hand-me-downs, good for her.

I settle back on the couch, watching the commotion whirl all around me. Dassi's kids are just like her — a perpetual wave of motion. My mother doesn't seem to mind at all. In fact, it looks like she's lapping up all the noise and good-natured bantering.

Her nest is almost empty. My sisters are all married, and my two brothers are away in yeshivah. I am the lone fledgling, but I am not enough. I know my mother is lonely. Her job goes a long way in filling that void, and so does the rotation we have of my sisters coming for Shabbos.

I sit there on the couch, feeling rather like a loner myself. I will for the phone to ring, wishing I could speak to someone, anyone.

But I know it won't ring — at least, not for me.

The girls in my class are wary to call Mrs. Bodner's house. I don't blame them. Who wants to have to speak to the principal outside of school? If I had a really close friend, no doubt she'd brave the discomfort and reach out to me even outside of the classroom walls.

I run my hand through my light-brown hair, sighing softly. I've got lots of "friendly friends," as befits The Principal's Daughter. I get along with everyone, and they get along with me. But a best friend, someone who understands me almost as well as I understand myself?

I have yet to meet her.

And though I am surrounded by family, and the conversation is ebbing and flowing as smoothly as the tide, I suddenly feel lonelier than I've ever felt before.

Atara

"ATARA! PHONE FOR YOU!" Janet's voice comes across loud and clear on the intercom.

I sigh and get up from Elisheva's bed, where I am reading yet another book to my little sisters. Our live-in's slightly hoarse voice never fails to grate on my nerves. I wonder if it's the way she pronounces my name so perfectly, without the slightest inflection of accent. For some reason, that bothers me — a lot.

Somehow, somewhere, over the years, Janet has become part of the fabric of our household, learning the nuances of *Yiddishkeit* and melding right into our lives. And though she is there by my parents' choice, at times it feels downright intrusive to me.

"Hello?" I say, picking up the phone and nestling it between my ear and shoulder.

"Don't talk so long," Esti entreats me, and I ruffle her feathery blonde hair. This is the third time we're being interrupted by the phone, and I feel bad.

"Hi, Atara," comes a familiar, slightly hesitant voice.

"Hi, Penina," I say. I look back toward the bed, where three little faces gaze earnestly at me. "I can't talk now. Can I call you back later?"

"Okay," Penina says agreeably. "Speak to you soon."

We hang up, and I head back to the bed, feeling slightly unsettled. I've never been good friends with Penina. She tends to hang around the edges of my group, an outsider looking in. I pride myself on being nice to everyone, gracious and accepting. But still…

I shrug slightly, then turn my attention back to the book — and my sisters.

Elisheva isn't so easily distracted, though. "Was that Malkie?" she asks.

I shake my head. "Nope."

"Yocheved?"

"Nope."

"Chana Rochel?"

Elisheva looks exasperated. It isn't any of the Big Three, so she's out of guesses. It's funny, but I'm happy that for once it isn't one of them. My friends are great, but lately I've been feeling like something is missing. They're fun and filled with personality, but…

I take a deep breath, not even noticing how my exhale comes out in a loud *whoosh*.

"What are you doing, Atara?" Miri asks, giggling.

Oops. I look guiltily at my sisters. They need me to be here with them now, not far away in my thoughts. I don't know why I'm thinking so much anyway. It's not really like me. It

20 • CURTAIN CALL

must be that I'm feeling unsettled with Mommy and Daddy so far away.

"Who wants to finish the book?" I ask, trying to sound cheerful.

"Who was on the phone?" Elisheva asks, refusing to be distracted.

"A girl named Penina," I say.

Elisheva frowns. "How come I never heard her name before?"

I don't know what to say. I don't know the answer myself — or actually, I do. It looks like Penina is becoming yet another girl trying to break into the inner circle surrounding Atara Gold.

And I can't say I like the thought of that one bit.

I look down at the book in my hands. There's a picture of a little girl in a blue dress, looking downcast. She reminds me of myself, although her red hair is so different from my own sleek blonde ponytail, and of course I'm much older.

I wonder, little girl. Are you also searching for a friend, a real friend, someone who cares about you and understands you? Someone who isn't running after you just because you live in a huge house and have anything a girl could ever want, plus more?

I sigh. I have everything I could ever want. And everything I never wanted.

I put the book down and gently close it. All I want to do right now is cry in the solitude of my lavender and pink bedroom.

Instead, I say Shema with my sisters while listening to the drone of the vacuum cleaner that Janet is running in the hallway.

CHAPTER 3

Brachie

THERE'S NO DOUBT ABOUT IT: Morah Bergman's Navi class is the best one of the day. Somehow, she manages to make the *perakim* come so *alive*. Dovid Hamelech running for his life, turning to Hashem, undergoing the worst kinds of *yissurim* known to mankind…

Morah Bergman likes to have us connect what we're learning with the *perek* of Tehillim composed at that time. I like that. It really makes Tehillim resonate so much more for me when I think about it against the backdrop of Tanach.

"Girls," Morah Bergman is saying, her voice passionate as usual, "Dovid Hamelech is fleeing. And who is chasing after him? His own son!"

Her voice echoes in the still classroom. We stare at her, electrified, hanging on to her every word.

And then comes the knock on the door.

Morah Bergman lowers her hands, disappointment on her face. Once a good lesson has been disturbed, it's almost impossible to get it fully back on track. I put down my pen, finding myself disappointed, too. Morah Bergman had been about to deliver the main crux of her lesson.

Around me, girls focus their attention on the doorway. Naomi Tusk, a twelfth grader, is standing there.

"Yes?" Morah Bergman asks.

"There's an assembly in the auditorium next period," Naomi says. She smiles apologetically. "The loudspeaker is broken."

A rustle of excitement is heard as girls start to fidget in their seats. Morah Bergman looks around the room, a frown on her face. Immediately, the movement is stilled.

But it's too late. The mood has been broken. Morah Bergman tries to pick up the momentum, but it's just not there anymore.

"As I was saying," Morah Bergman says resignedly, "Dovid Hamelech is running from his son..."

I try to imagine the king fleeing from his own flesh and blood. Instead, my mind keeps flitting to the upcoming assembly. Every so often, we are treated to guest speakers, handpicked by my mother. They're usually inspiring and entertaining, I have to admit. I know she works hard to find them.

I wonder who could be speaking to us today — and why my mother didn't mention anything to me.

Atara

I AM FLANKED, as usual, by Yocheved, Malkie, and Chana Rochel. A few other girls flutter around our periphery, like butterflies homing in on a target.

That target is me.

There was a time when that knowledge sent a delicious thrill through me, but lately I am feeling rather ambivalent about this. Are they after *me* — Atara Gold, possessor of *middos*, some good and some bad, but predominantly with a heart of gold (pun intended)? Or are they in pursuit of Atara Gold, daughter of Mr. Eli Gold, CEO of Gold Enterprises and one of the richest men in the city?

I wonder. And the unsettling feeling I am left with is not one I want to dwell on.

Instead, I turn to Yocheved, my brightest smile on my face. "So," I say, "any idea what this assembly is all about?"

Yocheved shakes her head, her dainty gold hoops swaying slightly.

"Who cares?" Malkie says, smoothing out her perfectly pleated skirt. "As long as we miss class, what does it matter?"

I laugh along with my friends. Assemblies — especially unplanned ones — are most welcome events in Bais Breindel.

I nod absently at my friends from other grades. Most of them live in Windsor Hills, like me, in museum-like homes with manicured lawns. Our parents are friends, members of the same social stratosphere.

Tziri Cohen catches my eye. Her mother has been my mother's best friend for years, and we're used to sharing Shabbos *seudos* together. Tziri is only one year younger than me, but I can tell she is awed by my sophomore status. I adjust my thick navy headband and smile benevolently in her direction. Then I slide onto a bench, my friends at either side of me like well-placed bookends.

Mrs. Bodner steps up to the microphone, and a hush falls over the enormous room. I marvel at the way our principal has a way of commanding automatic respect.

I search her face, wondering why she has called this assembly. She doesn't look particularly serious, which is a good sign. In fact, her eyes are twinkling behind her rimless glasses, and her mouth is turning up in a smile.

"I'm going to hand the floor right over to Morah Bulman," she says.

I exchange an excited glance with Yocheved. This is getting better and better! Morah Bulman is the twelfth-grade *mechaneches* and head of extracurricular activities.

I lean forward in my seat as Morah Bulman takes Mrs. Bodner's place up at the microphone, her short brown *sheitel* bobbing.

"Well," she says slowly, looking around the room. She smiles broadly, and I can almost feel the charge of anticipation spreading through the room. "I have an announcement to make…but you know what they say." She winks. "A picture is worth a thousand words!"

I watch expectantly as the curtains draped over the stage are slowly pulled back. An enormous screen is set up. Someone turns off the lights in the auditorium, and the room explodes in song.

I sit up straight, my heart pounding. I recognize the song playing. It's from…

"Production!" Malkie squeals.

We watch as scenes from last year's production flash across the screen. I strain for a glimpse of myself.

"There's me!" Yocheved says proudly as the camera zooms in on her solo.

All around us, girls are clapping and cheering. The entire community — not to mention us students — looks forward each year to Bais Breindel's annual production. It's a really professional performance, complete with a spellbinding play, choirs, dances, scenery, props — the works!

I hug myself, fairly tingling with excitement. I can almost see the spotlights shining in my eyes, a kaleidoscope of vivid color. Some girls are born to perform — and I'm one of them.

"This is so exciting!" Chana Rochel squeals as the slideshow winds to an end.

"We've got to make the most of it," Malkie, ever practical, says wisely.

The lights come back on. I rub my eyes, feeling like I've just taken a brief but amazing trip to the world of the stage.

"So girls," Morah Bulman says, scanning her audience, "are you ready for production?"

A resounding cheer is all the answer she needs.

"Great! Then let's get down to business." Morah Bulman looks down at the paper in her hands. "Heads of production this year are…"

A drum roll sounds as we all get in the spirit.

"Tirtza Lorch and Suri Davis!"

The twelfth graders erupt in cheers. I clap loudly as Morah Bulman announces the rest of the heads. True to Bais Breindel tradition, they are all twelfth graders.

Chana Rochel's next words tug me right back to the matter

at hand. "So," she says eagerly, "what's everyone going to try out for?"

Yocheved is the first to jump into the discussion, but we all know her answer to the question already. With a voice as smooth as butter, she's a favored soloist whenever she performs.

Malkie would like to be in dance, of course, and Chana Rochel in ensemble.

"And you, Atara?" Malkie asks.

I smile dreamily. In some schools, the girls clamor to be in dance. In others, choir takes central stage. But in Bais Breindel, the entire production centers around the play. They are usually so well constructed and performed that people talk about it for weeks, even months, afterward.

"Me?" I say, as if the answer is obvious. "I want to be in drama."

Brachie

OF COURSE! How could I not have guessed the obvious? With February looming just a few short months away, I'm not sure why Morah Bulman's announcement catches me so off-guard.

But I do know something: I'm just as excited about it as everyone else.

I am mesmerized as scenes from Bais Breindel's last production flash across the stage. I may not be Miss Outgoing or Miss Personality, but it's undeniable that I have a flair for drama. I certainly get enough practice. As The Principal's Daughter, am I not always on stage, with my actions and behavior constantly being evaluated? Do I not smile when I want to cry, and keep my head high when all I want to do is cuddle under my blanket in the privacy of my room?

As Morah Bulman announces that Ricki Kaplan and Zehava Yarmush are this year's heads of drama, I dream about landing a coveted role in the play... I will ace the tryouts, wowing everyone right away... This will be the opportunity I've been waiting for!

I will not be seen as The Principal's Daughter now, nor even as just another girl reading the same old lines. My audition will be so breathtaking that whoever hears it will forget I have any relationship whatsoever with Mrs. Bodner. They will see me only as Brachie Bodner, actress extraordinaire.

I am smiling victoriously as I sail out of the auditorium, streams of excited chatter filling my ears. Then I reach the wide entrance to the room. That's when I spot my mother, talking animatedly to Morah Bulman.

My smile freezes, then fades altogether. I have suddenly realized a rather minute detail that sends my heady daydream sailing right out the window.

How could the heads of drama assign a starring role to The Principal's Daughter? Wouldn't everyone view that as favoritism, or nepotism, or something equally horrid?

Besides, would they even *want* me as part of the cast?

My mother catches my eye and smiles. It's all I can do to nod and try to smile back.

CHAPTER 4

Atara

Tonight, not even the fact that Mommy isn't home can get under my skin. I am too busy soaring along the wings of my dreams.

I see myself, center stage, transporting the audience to new worlds, better realms. I can practically hear the adoring comments cast my way.

"Atara, you were amazing!" is ringing in my ears, blotting out the mundane sounds of the here and now. That's why it takes me a few minutes to realize that Janet is holding out the phone that has been ringing right next to me.

"Oh!" I say, flushing.

Janet looks at me oddly but says nothing.

"Hello?"

"Atara, honey, is that you?"

"Mommy!" I come back to earth with a thud. "How's your trip going?"

"Wonderful!" my mother says, sounding relaxed and carefree. "It's so beautiful here in Italy. I've been snapping pictures left and right."

I sit back on the kitchen chair, fiddling with the cutlery that Janet has neatly laid out.

"Uh-huh," I say absently. I pick up a spoon and ogle at my distorted reflection. My bright green eyes look tiny, and my high cheekbones seem to have fallen. I wrinkle my nose and put the spoon back on the table.

"So how are the girls doing?" my mother asks.

I can hear my sisters squabbling in the basement playroom. They usually get along pretty well, but I know my parents' vacation is hard for them. Poor girls.

"Fine, *baruch Hashem*," I reply, for lack of a better response.

"Wonderful," my mother says again. "Is everything working out at home?"

"Sure." I shrug, even though my mother can't see me. Janet keeps our house running like clockwork, as she always does. My parents' absence doesn't make such a difference in that sense — except that they're not home, and there's a void in our home that no sense of order can dispel.

I swallow. "Guess what?" I say, veering to a more favorable topic. "Production tryouts are this week!"

"Really?" My mother sounds excited. She knows how much this means to me. "So, let me guess...are you going to try out for drama queen?"

I laugh. That's a standing joke in my house. I was an only child until I was seven, and my parents tell me I was quite spoiled. All I had to do was pout or pretend to be upset, and I got whatever I wanted. My father fondly called me a "drama queen," and the nickname stuck.

"I'm really nervous," I confide. "There are so many great actresses out there."

"But there's only one Atara Gold," my mother says smoothly.

I smile, secure in the knowledge that my mother believes in me — and then I freeze. Does she mean that she has faith in my acting abilities? Or…or does she mean that I'm bound to get the part I want because my father is the CEO of Gold Enterprises?

I can hear my sisters thundering up the stairs.

"Mommy, the girls want to talk to you," I say quickly. I stumble through my goodbyes and allow Elisheva to grab the phone from my hand. Then I flee upstairs to my room, although Janet is already removing supper — courtesy of Tziri Cohen's mother — from the oven.

How can I eat, when a thousand questions are drumming through my head?

Brachie

THE SOUND OF THE PIANO POUNDING is the first thing I hear when I walk into the house. I wonder who is making all that noise. My mother likes to play music sometimes, but this cacophony can only be made by…

"Yaakov!" I exclaim, catching sight of my nephew.

"Hi, Brachie," my sister Ettie greets me.

"Hi," I say as I put my knapsack down in its spot. "What are you doing here?"

"Mommy invited us for supper tonight."

I smile. I like when my sisters come over for short visits that won't result in the total disarray of our house. I hold out my hands to my tiny niece, who is half asleep in her mother's arms.

"How's school?" Ettie asks me.

I smile wryly. Ettie is the most like me of all my sisters — reserved and restrained, and not as pumped with confidence. I know that she didn't have the easiest time when my mother taught her class — and she understands, at least to some degree, that life as The Principal's Daughter is not all peaches and cream.

"Actually," I say, perking up, "today they announced that production tryouts will be this week!"

Ettie grins. "That's so much fun!"

I cock my head, mulling that over. To me, performing isn't *fun*. It's an art, an opportunity, an experience.

Ettie sits down on the piano bench next to Yaakov. "Do you want me to play you a real song?" she asks.

"I *is* playing real song!" Yaakov protests indignantly.

We burst out laughing, and I cuddle my baby niece tightly.

"You know, Ettie…" I begin, turning serious. I want to ask her if she thinks being The Principal's Daughter is going to count against me, if the heads will be hesitant to include me… or if perhaps the reverse will transpire: will they feel *obligated* to accept me? Will everyone think they assigned me a role because they had no choice?

Not that that happened last year, of course, but then…then there were extenuating circumstances.

I take a deep breath and try to formulate my worries into coherent words. But...my mother chooses just that moment to come into the room.

"Hi, Brachie," she says. "I didn't hear you come in."

"I just walked in," I reply, feeling slightly guilty.

"How was your day?" she asks. She laughs. "At least, the part that I wasn't there for."

I smile, although I don't think it's at all funny. Ettie looks at me, understanding in her eyes.

"Brachie was telling me about production," she tells my mother.

I am sending her warning glances, but she doesn't catch them. I don't want to discuss production — and the dreams I have for it — with my mother. I am desperate to hold onto a corner of my life that is just mine, without my mother knowing all about it.

"We have a really great script for this year," my mother says animatedly. "We had an excellent book written up as a play — and I know everyone is going to love it!"

"Which book?" I ask, forgetting that I hadn't wanted to talk about production.

My mother smiles mysteriously. "I don't want to ruin the suspense."

"Aww, Ima!" I pout. "You know I won't tell anyone."

I know I sound like I have the maturity level of a second grader, but right now I don't care. I am desperate to find out which book our production will revolve around.

"You'll find out tomorrow," my mother says. "Tryouts are after school, so —" she looks at her watch — "you only have about another twenty-four hours to go."

"Ima," I say disappointedly, as Ettie laughs.

I frown at Ettie. Doesn't she realize what's at stake here? If I only knew which book our production was based on, I could plan accordingly. I could imagine myself in that time period, mentally review the main characters, step into their lives... and come to the audition that much more prepared. The fact that that might not be so fair eludes me at the moment.

My mother stifles a yawn. "I'm tired," she murmurs. "I'm going to go finish up supper."

Ettie jumps up as Yaakov bangs loudly on the piano keys. "I'll help you, Mommy."

I watch my mother leave the room, Ettie at her heels. My mother is so tired lately, no doubt from the pressures of her job. She has so little time to rest, too, between hosting my married sisters all the time and attending *simchos* of former students.

Maybe this week we should have an "off Shabbos," without any of my siblings in attendance. Although they liven up the house, my sisters and their families keep my mother — and me — moving about nonstop. By the time they leave, I often wish I could just crawl into bed myself.

I make a mental note to suggest this to my mother as soon as Ettie leaves the house.

"I'm going up to my room, Yaakov," I say. "Wanna come with me?"

He slides off the piano bench and tucks his little hand inside my own. I shift little Bassie to a more secure position in my arm as I pick up my knapsack and head upstairs.

It's time do some homework...and to dream.

Atara

THIS TIME, when the phone jangles, I catch it on the first ring.

I am sitting at my custom-made desk that juts into a corner of my room at perfect right angles. My desk is one of my favorite parts of my room. I can swivel my chair from side to side, and I have plenty of space to spread out all my stuff.

Right now, the pale purple surface of the desk is covered with papers and notebooks. I grimace. The woes of homework!

I focus on the phone, from which I hear Malkie saying, "Atara?"

"That's me," I reply, laughing. Who else would it be?

"My sister told me..."

I sit upright, all ears. Malkie's sister is a twelfth grader and one of the heads of dance.

"This year's play is going to be — one second," Malkie interrupts herself. I can hear her muffled voice in the background. She comes back on a moment later. "Sorry. What was I saying?"

"The play," I say, a bit tersely. How could she leave me dangling like that?

"Right," Malkie says. "I figured you'd want to know."

"Want to know *what*?" I am fairly quivering with impatience.

"About the play," Malkie says. I am about to command her to just tell me what she wants to say already, but I hold my tongue. Patience is a virtue, I remind myself. "My sister said it's based on a really good book. She said — one minute."

I grit my teeth as Malkie's voice fades into the background again.

"Sorry," she apologizes again. "Shaina said she thinks it's going to be the best play ever. The book is one everyone knows, and she's already come up with some really good ideas for dance."

"Which book is the play based on?" I ask eagerly.

"She didn't say."

I can almost see Malkie shrug. I am annoyed. She called to tell me that the play is based on a book — but she doesn't even know which book? That doesn't give me much to go on.

I sigh. If only I could be privy to this top-secret knowledge, I could have an edge at auditions. Perhaps the book is one sitting on my own bookshelf. What more worthy pursuit than to spend the night re-reading it, getting to know the characters intimately — and picturing how I'd represent them myself?

"Oh," is all I say to my friend. "Well, thanks for letting me know about this."

"No problem!" Malkie sounds pleased with herself. "This is so exciting, isn't it?"

I nod. "Yup, it really is."

And I mean it. I just wish she would've been able to share something more with me — something that would've helped me land the role I want so badly.

CHAPTER 5

Brachie

THE ATMOSPHERE IN THE HALLWAY is both subdued and charged at the same time. There is an undercurrent of excitement laced with anxiety as girls chat in low voices, their expressions serious.

Tonight is the night.

Tonight we will stand before the twelfth-grade heads, give them our best…and then exit the room, practically leaving our fate in their hands.

The thought is not a particularly pleasant one.

I am standing next to Tzippy Berg and Devora Kenig. We are waiting for the drama heads to open the classroom door where they are busy conferring, and fill us in on this year's script. Down the hall, I can see long lines of girls waiting to try out for dance. The other tryouts are taking place a floor above us.

"All girls waiting for drama, come on in," Zehava Yarmush finally says, flinging open the door. Behind her, Ricki Kaplan eyes the girls who filter in. Both girls look excited, but nervous. The responsibility of picking a good cast — the best cast — is a big one. The success of the play hinges on it.

I take a seat in the middle of the room. I don't want to look too anxious by sitting in the front, nor do I want to seem disinterested by heading toward the back. I look around the room, curious to know who else from my class is trying out for drama. Besides for Tzippy and Devora, I see Bayla Beck and Atara Gold. Atara looks awfully anxious, and I wonder why.

She had a pretty big role in last year's performance, and everyone knows she's a great actress. So why the solemn expression?

I turn my attention to Zehava and Ricki, who are standing behind the teacher's desk. They seem so grown-up and professional, more like teachers than the seniors they really are.

"Okay," Zehava says loudly, and that one word is all it takes for silence to envelop the room. "This year's play…"

"…is going to be the best ever!" Ricki finishes, grinning.

We all clap automatically.

Zehava picks up a stack of scripts and looks around the room. "Most of you have probably heard of the book *With Hearts of Fire*."

I nod, along with many other girls. Sure, I know the book. It's about a family who escapes from Spain during the Inquisition.

"Our play is going to be based on that book," Zehava continues. She motions to the papers in her arms. "We're handing out Scene Three, Act One. You'll have about fifteen minutes to read these pages over, and then we're going to have girls read different lines aloud."

Right now my own heart feels like it's on fire. I remember being mesmerized by that book when I read it a few years ago. The main character is a teenage girl who must flee from Spain with her sister after her parents are arrested. I cried over the story, and I am itching now to play the part of the heroine, Gracia.

I take the sheaf of papers passed to me, hardly realizing what I am doing. All I can imagine is looking at the cast list… and seeing my name right beside the leading role.

Atara

FIFTEEN MINUTES.

That's all we have to peruse the lines that will decide our future. Perhaps I sound melodramatic, but that's the right of the drama queen, is it not?

The seconds are trickling away like the grains of sand in an hourglass. I pore over the sheets as if my life depends on it. I remember *With Hearts of Fire*, though not as well as I wish I did.

Right now my entire body feels like it's on fire, as I sit on the edge of my seat with my heart racing wildly.

I scan the lines of the main character, imagining myself as the noble Gracia. I can fairly see myself sweeping across the stage, ready to forsake everything for the opportunity to truly serve Hashem.

"Okay," Zehava says, interrupting my daydream, "we're now going to call randomly on girls to read some lines."

CURTAIN CALL • 39

I frown. This is so different from how tryouts were run last year. Then, each girl went into the room to try out by herself, with only the heads in attendance. I don't like the idea of a whole roomful of girls watching me try out. It seems intrusive, somehow.

Ricki motions to a ninth grader to come to the front of the room. The girl stands up, looking scared. My heart goes out to her.

"Turn to the second page," Ricki tells her. "Go to Francesca's lines, where she says, 'But Gracia, I'm frightened.'"

The girl obeys. I can see her fingers trembling as she turns the page.

"I'm going to read Gracia's lines right before, and then you're going to say Francesca's part."

The ninth grader nods, looking tense.

"We have no choice," Ricki says earnestly, her eyes darting around the room. "We must leave Spain. Mama, Papa — they've been taken, Francesca. We're next — can't you see?"

My eyes are upon the poor girl, the first victim of tonight's audition.

"But Gracia," she says, her voice wobbling, "I am frightened."

Despite my tension, I have to stifle a smile. This girl certainly doesn't have to act to sound frightened. I listen as Ricki instructs her to read several more lines, then chooses another girl to try out.

I mentally rate the ninth grader's performance as I watch Zehava scribbling down some notes. She wasn't bad, but she wasn't great either. I do not view her as formidable competition.

My fingers absently drum the desk in front of me as Ricki

picks two other girls to read their lines together. I think that's a good idea — you can really get a feel for how an actress will relate to the other people in the play when they audition together.

The girls fumble through their lines, looking uncertain. I feel guiltily gratified when Zehava makes a few quick notations in her notebook — no doubt they will not be included in the cast list.

I am just starting to relax in my seat, content to watch other girls audition while hoping that my own turn is a long way off, when Ricki looks directly at me.

"Atara," she says, "can you come to the front of the room?"

Brachie

BRILLIANT.

There is no other way to describe Atara Gold's performance. She begs Devora Kenig — who is assuming the role of Gracia at the moment — to stay in Spain.

"I can't," she whimpers, sounding like she is on the verge of tears. "I'm so scared. Please, Gracia. Let's stay here. We can hide in Dona Esperanza's house…we can pretend to be her nieces from abroad…we can…" Atara looks down at the papers in her hand and giggles nervously. "Sorry," she says to Ricki. "I got carried away. I wasn't following the lines exactly."

"That's okay," Ricki murmurs, looking in awe at Atara.

I am mesmerized myself, certain that Atara Gold has just landed the main role in the play. The entire room seems charged with the electricity of her performance.

I watch as Ricki tells Atara and Devora to flip forward a

few more pages and read some more lines. The setting has changed, the conversation is different...and still, Atara sweeps us along with the power of her performance.

"Okay," Ricki says, "thanks. That's enough."

Devora slides into the seat beside mine, looking nervous. I give her a reassuring smile.

"You were great," I whisper. I mean it, too. But it's obvious that she came nowhere near Atara's grand performance.

"Brachie," Ricki says, looking at me. "Can you come up now?"

Is it my imagination, or does she phrase that request differently, hesitantly? I am instantly sucked into the vacuum of despair, engendered by my role as The Principal's Daughter.

I think of lucky Atara, who is practically guaranteed a starring role. She will not have to wonder if she landed the role because of any external factors.

I sigh as I make my way to the front of the room.

"Turn to page four," Ricki instructs me when I am standing next to her.

I take a deep breath and obey.

"You are going to read Gracia's lines, when she tells Francesca why they must run away," Ricki tells me.

I am tense and edgy. My heart is pounding so quickly, I wonder how I will get any words out. I want to cry, to bolt out of the room. This is already a nightmare, and I haven't even opened my mouth.

Standing there, a roomful of eyes trained on me, I am catapulted back to last year's production tryouts. I remember standing in front of the all-knowing drama heads, girls from last year's senior class, knowing that I *could* act, that I *was* blessed with a flair for drama, when I was seized by intense fear. I could barely get the lines out of my quivering lips, and they fell flatter than a cake without baking powder. It was the most humiliating, most horrible experience.

Hashem, please help me, I murmur urgently. *Please don't let this be a repeat of last year.*

It is then that I see two eleventh graders in the front row eying me intently. They are whispering to each other, and I catch the words, "Mrs. Bodner's daughter."

That does it.

"Page four," I say tersely, feeling like I am going out to war. I will show those girls — I will show *everyone* — just what Brachie Bodner is all about. She is a whole lot more than just "Mrs. Bodner's daughter!"

I open my mouth, and the words tumble out with all the emotion and turmoil that is roiling in my own heart.

"We have no choice, Francesca!" I cry, willing my pretend sister to understand. "If we stay here, we could be killed. And even if we merit to live, what type of life will we have? What *is* life without Torah and mitzvos, dear sister?"

I stop and wait for Mimi Kahn, who is reading Francesca's lines, to answer. My cheeks are flushed and my head is hammering.

"Okay," Ricki says. "Now I want you to go to the next page, where Francesca and Gracia are arguing. This time, Brachie, you read Francesca's lines. Mimi, you'll play Gracia."

I nod and flip to the next page. I am aware of the many pairs of eyes upon me. My heart pounds, and I feel weak suddenly.

"Gracia," I say, my voice dropping to a whisper, "I'm so scared." *I'm so scared,* I think desperately. *What if I don't land a big part?* "I just keep thinking…what if they catch us? What if…"

"Life is filled with 'what if's,' Francesca," Mimi says gently.

"I know," I say miserably. "But that doesn't make me feel any better!" I feel like wailing, and my voice ends off on a high pitch. Oops. I did *not* mean for that to happen.

"Okay, thanks," Ricki says. "That's it."

I'm finished. I head back to my seat, filled with the sense that *something* just happened here in this classroom…but I'm not really sure what.

Atara

MAGICAL.

I stare at Brachie, as if seeing her for the first time. I had no idea she was so talented.

I listen to her convince "Francesca" that they must leave Spain so they can lead life as true Jews. Of course, I should not be shocked at how well she conveys those sentiments. She is Mrs. Bodner's daughter, after all. Has she not been reared on Torah-true *hashkafos* her whole life? Still, I am amazed that she is such a good actress.

I feel that my own audition went well. Ricki seemed satisfied, and I saw Zehava nodding approvingly. But as I watch Brachie take over the room with the sheer magnetism of her performance, I feel doubt worm its way into my mind.

She is truly a remarkable actress. I am happy for her, I tell myself.

But if she lands the starring role…where will that leave me?

CHAPTER 6

Brachie

Deep brown eyes stare back at me from the ornate mirror in the front hallway. The eyes are mine. The entire face — finely chiseled features, slightly angular nose, and jutting cheekbones — is as familiar as always.

And yet, something is different. There is a sparkle in my eyes that I haven't seen in a long time. My whole face seems uplifted, somehow.

"How'd it go tonight?" my mother asks, leaning over the banister.

I tear my eyes away from my reflection and look upstairs.

"Good, *baruch Hashem*."

Those words are too sparse to encapsulate what I want to say: *Ima, it was amazing! I really did my best. But...what if they don't want me anyway? What if they decide it's not a good idea to give The Principal's Daughter a big role? What if all my efforts were for nothing?*

I allow myself a small smile as I remember a line from the play: "Life is filled with 'what if's.'"

"Were there a lot of girls trying out?" my mother asks.

I'm not sure if she's truly curious or just trying to make conversation.

I nod. "Yeah, the halls were filled."

I am itching to confide in my mother, to ask her if she thinks my status as a Bodner is going to work against me. But I say nothing. I am worried my mother will speak to the drama heads; worried that somehow she will get involved behind the scenes and then everything will fall apart.

I start climbing up the stairs. It is only then that I notice my mother is wearing a robe.

"Going to sleep already?" I ask.

"Soon." My mother stifles a yawn, then smiles reproachfully. "I've really been putting in way too many hours. When will I remember that I'm not as young as I used to be?"

I stare at her. My mother isn't *that* old! I've never heard her speak like that before, and I'm suddenly worried.

That's when I remember the idea I had yesterday, when Ettie was at our house. I'd forgotten to broach it to my mother.

"I was thinking," I say. I pause, not sure how my mother will react. My mother looks expectantly at me, and I plow on. "Maybe we shouldn't have any guests this week," I say. "I mean, you're so tired and all…"

My mother is already shaking her head. "My children aren't guests!" she insists. "Besides, I already invited Shifra and Chevy ages ago."

My heart sinks. "Shifra *and* Chevy are coming?"

My mother nods, a smile lighting up her face. She is no doubt thinking of all the *nachas* moments she will derive from their small children.

I, on the other hand, am thinking of all the noise and chaos.

I look guiltily at my mother, hoping she cannot read my thoughts. I enjoy my sisters' company, and I adore my nieces and nephews. But there are times when I wish we could have a quiet, slow Shabbos with no one else around.

The phone rings, and my mother turns to get it.

"Dassi was supposed to call me back," she says.

I continue to my room. I have homework to finish, and a Chumash test I'd like to start studying for.

But try as I might, I can think of only one thing.

Ricki and Zehava told us they'd be hanging up the cast list on Monday. I cannot begin to imagine how I'll be able to wait that long.

Atara

"ATARA!" Yocheved's voice comes through loud and clear on the phone. She sounds happy, giddy almost.

"Hi!" I say, plopping onto my perfectly-made bed. "How'd it go?"

"Great," Yocheved says flippantly. "I sang a few songs, and that was it. How about you?"

No wonder she sounds so happy. Yocheved *knows* she's got an entrance ticket right into choir — not to mention a few guaranteed solos.

"Me?" I say slowly. "It went okay, I think."

"C'mon, Atara! We all know you're a great actress."

I smile. "Well, it *did* go okay. But other girls were also great."

"I'm sure you'll get a main role," Yocheved says. She titters. "You're Atara Gold, after all."

I am instantly on edge. What does she mean by that?

"So what?" I say, trying to feel her out. "What does that have to do with anything?"

"You have a reputation as an amazing actress," Yocheved says.

I'm not at all convinced that's what she means, but I decide not to pursue it. I'm feeling tired of this conversation. I wonder what's wrong with me. Why am I second-guessing myself and those around me so much lately?

Yocheved changes the topic to the social studies report we were just assigned, and I try to show some interest. It's hard, though. My head is back in the classroom where I auditioned just an hour ago.

Brachie

IT'S ANTICLIMACTIC, SOMEHOW, to walk through the wide front doors of Bais Breindel when I had exited them, flushed with such headiness, only the night before.

I look automatically toward the large bulletin board hanging next to the office, but, aside for a few odd notices, it's empty. I know that the results of the tryouts won't be posted until next week, but I am disappointed nonetheless.

I swing my knapsack onto my back and head toward my

locker on the second floor. On the way, I pass Ricki Kaplan, head of drama. She hardly looks in my direction, and I feel a pit settle in my stomach.

If she were going to choose me as one of her leading actresses, wouldn't she have acknowledged my presence with at least a nod? The knowledge that this does not bode well does nothing for my mood.

"Hi, Brachie," I hear someone say.

I look up, my lips stretching reflexively into a polite smile. It's Devora.

She attempts to make small chat, but it's all I can do to just nod at the appropriate intervals.

I open my locker and take out the *sefarim* I will need until recess. I am banging the door closed when I see Atara Gold coming down the hall.

She is tall and poised, as usual, and I am filled with an uncomfortable sensation as she comes ever closer.

Some people are born with a silver spoon in their mouths, and Atara is one of them. Always surrounded by admirers, always assured of her position at the head of the class's hierarchy, has Atara ever experienced a moment of insecurity?

I am not one to let these things get to me, but the fact that Atara is almost certain to garner the leading role makes me unable to look her in the face now. Yes, I know that, despite her lofty social status, she is a sweet, well-meaning girl. But at this moment, I can't focus on that. I am consumed by jealousy, and I'm upset — and it's not even Atara I'm upset at.

I'm disgusted with myself.

Atara

I WONDER, as I walk down the school halls, if Brachie Bodner is as uncomfortable to see me as I am to see her. There were quite a few girls in our class who tried out for drama, but none of them acted as magnificently as did Brachie.

True, there were plenty of other great actresses last night. There was an eleventh grader who fairly sparkled through her lines, and a ninth grader who had me at the edge of my seat.

But Brachie is a fellow sophomore, one of "my own." That makes me feel somewhat threatened by her, though I know it's silly of me to think that way.

I sigh and clutch my knapsack a little tighter. I am the drama queen. I am used to my parents giving me whatever I want. I know my friends will do whatever I tell them. And yet, I *need* to land the starring role in the school play. I want to be acknowledged for my talent, not for my designer knapsack or sprawling house. I want to be lauded for my own abilities, and not for my parents' bank account. Knowing that I truly count in that way will fill up the empty spaces in me like nothing else can.

And that's why I can hardly look at Brachie as I notice her standing next to her locker. I am relieved that she doesn't see me.

I like Brachie — I really do. She's one of those all-around great girls whom I look up to and respect. But I saw the rapture in the heads' eyes as they watched her perform. I saw how the entire room was spellbound as she swept through her lines.

And I am afraid, so terribly frightened, that the part I want so badly will go to Brachie.

To my shame, I continue right past her, without even saying hello.

Brachie

I AM TAKEN BY SURPRISE when the door opens at the start of recess and Ricki Kaplan walks inside. My classmates, who are busy conversing, fall silent as they eye the twelfth grader. She scans the classroom, then looks down at a piece of paper in her hand.

Her eyes light up when she sees Atara. My heart plunges to the soles of my leather loafers.

"Atara," Ricki says, smiling in her direction, "can I borrow you for a few moments?"

Atara looks confused, then gratified. I am hot, then cold, as I realize what this means.

Atara is being summoned for something that has to do with production — and I am *not*.

Ricki is still looking around the classroom. I can see Devora eying her hopefully from her corner. I am sure my expression is just as anxious.

After several nerve-wracking seconds, Ricki's eyes fall on me.

"Brachie?" she says. "Can you come with me, too?"

I nod, unable to say anything else. I can feel my cheeks flame, and my hands are trembling slightly. I ball them into fists, trying to regain my composure.

I am aware of the silence in the classroom as my classmates watch me join Ricki and Atara. Then the door swings shut behind us, and I imagine the room becoming swamped with noise once again, with everyone discussing what this latest turn of events could mean. I vacillate between sweet anticipation and intense fright.

What is going on?

Ricki turns to us. "Zehava and I wanted to hear the two of you read some more lines," she says. "We want to get a feel for which actresses will go well together."

I feel a surge of hope. So they didn't compose the cast list yet. And they're interested in me, Brachie Bodner!

My heart lurches the next moment. How will I handle the strain of more tryouts? The anxious tension, the worry and fears?

Ricki looks at me. "It'll only take a few minutes," she says.

I blush, embarrassed that my thoughts are so transparent. I stand as straight as I can, trying to exude confidence as befits The Principal's Daughter.

It's no use. The moment we walk into the library, where these impromptu re-tryouts are being held, my knees can barely support me. About fifteen girls are there, much less than there were during the first round of tryouts.

That is a good sign, I know. This room is holding the best of the actresses from last night. Most of the girls in this room will garner leading roles in the play.

Most of them.

Not all of them.

And there is only one starring role.

Atara

THERE'S ONLY ONE starring role.

Of course, there are other major roles, too, but none that will elicit the same admiration as the noble Gracia.

I look around the room, taking in the faces around me. The other girls are mostly older, and all performed magnificently during tryouts. There are two timid-looking ninth graders. Brachie and I are the only tenth graders.

I recoil slightly at the thought.

Why would they assign a leading role to a younger girl? Wouldn't they rather give it to an older, more confident student?

I reassure myself that I am Atara Gold, and that counts for something. Then I peek at Brachie. She is Mrs. Bodner's daughter, and maybe that counts for more?

I fold my arms, then unfold them and stand straight, trying to look as confident as possible. I will not let anyone get a peek at the insecurities pecking at me.

"Okay," Zehava says. "We don't have too much time. I told Morah Bulman we wouldn't be more than a few minutes late to the next class." She nods at Tali Rein, a tall eleventh grader. "Can you read the lines of Maria, on this page?" She motions to Sara Sorchert. "And you play the role of the other maid, here." She points to some lines on the script she hands to Sara.

I watch the girls read their lines, begrudging admiration in my eyes. They are both good, really good. They say their lines as if they are truly back in the Spain of long ago, plotting the downfall of a devout Jewish family.

I carefully watch their facial expressions, their movements, the rise and fall of their voices, looking to see what I can incorporate into my own audition. I am admiring how Sara has a way of enunciating certain syllables to get just the right dramatic effect, when Ricki says, "Okay, I think that's enough. Thank you, Tali and Sara. Atara and Brachie, can you read those same lines?"

I peek at Brachie as she looks at me, and then we both slowly head to the front of the room.

CHAPTER 7

Brachie

INSECURITY.

It wracks me as I stumble through my classes, not really listening to what the teachers are saying. It haunts me as I walk home through the frigid streets, the bare branches of the trees bobbing forlornly. It follows me into my house, where I am confronted by the dark, desolate interior.

I frown as I look around. It's so unlike my mother not to be home at this time of day. Instantly, thoughts of production and this morning's re-tryouts fly out of my mind. I am focused on only one thing: where is my mother?

"Ima?" I call warily.

Although I am already fifteen, it is as if ten years of my life have just been shaved away. Suddenly, I'm a little girl again, desperate for the comfort only a mother can provide.

"Ima?" I try again, my voice louder.

The phone rings loudly, breaking the stillness. I pounce on it, hoping it will offer some clue as to my mother's whereabouts.

"Hi, Brachie?" Dassi's cheerful voice echoes in my ear.

"Dassi!" I say her name as if it's a lifeline. "Do you know —"

Suddenly, I can hear another receiver being picked up. Cold fear freezes my muscles, and goose-bumps prick me like a porcupine's taut quills. Who else is in this house?

"Dassi?" I hear my mother's voice, sounding slightly muffled.

"Ima?" Dassi and I say together. My voice is shrill and nearly drowns out my sister's.

"Are you okay, Brachie?" my sister asks.

"Why are you home, Brachie?" my mother wonders, her voice echoing slightly in my ear.

"Why am I home?" My voice is rising, sounding panicky, and I force myself to calm down. "It's five-thirty already, Ima."

"Oh." Ima sounds confused. "I guess I overslept."

Dassi laughs, sounding amused. "Brachie, why don't you go talk to Ima in person? I'll call back later."

I am decidedly not amused as I hang up the phone and trudge up the stairs. I flick on lights as I pass fixtures, and suddenly the dark house seems much less threatening. My mother must have fallen asleep when it was still light outside, I realize. But why did she take such a long nap in the middle of the day?

The questions and doubts clamor in my head as my mother comes out of her room, rubbing her eyes and yawning.

"Sorry about that, Brachie," she says. She looks down at her watch ruefully. "You're probably hungry for supper."

Food is the least of my concerns at the moment. "Why are you so tired, Ima?" I ask worriedly. "Are you feeling okay?"

She shrugs. "Too much work, I guess." She yawns again. "I'm going to heat up some of the leftovers from last night. It should be ready soon."

I follow my mother downstairs, as if keeping her in sight will make sure she's really fine.

"Abba called before to say he's coming home early tonight," my mother says. "It's a good thing I have enough food left over. I was going to make meatballs, but I never got around to it." She sighs as she puts a few covered pans inside the oven.

"I can make the meatballs," I offer. "They don't take long, right?"

My mother smiles. "You're a good girl, Brachie," she murmurs. "But it's okay. I'll make them tomorrow night. You probably want to get a head start on your homework, don't you?"

I do, actually. I am a high achiever in my schoolwork — as I am with the rest of my life. But right now, I can't evince any interest in my social studies homework or upcoming math test.

Is it true what my mother is saying? Is she really just overworked?

Or is it something else — something much worse — that is wrong?

Atara

People say my home is gorgeous. Magnificent, some call it. And it is. My mother hired a team of interior decorators to make sure our house would resemble a mini palace.

But right now, all the exquisite trappings, all the stunning luxury, can't fill the emptiness that hovers over the brightly-lit hallways. Without parents to turn our house into a home, what's the point of it all?

Perhaps I am being melodramatic, as drama queens can sometimes be. But I am aching to speak to my mother, to tell her about today's re-tryouts and exactly how they went. I'm sure she would want to hear about them...except that she's on the other side of the ocean.

I know my parents will be home in just a few days, and the thought fills me with relief. But it's hard to sit here alone in my room — even if that room is a girl's dream come true — and yearn for my parents to step through the front door and just *be* my parents.

I remember when I was a little girl, an only child, and how my parents doted on me. We were well-off, but not in the wealthy way that defines our lifestyle today. My father hardly ever had to travel for business, and my mother was around almost whenever I wanted her.

Today we have anything we could want, a stunning house with a live-in to maintain it, beautiful clothes, the latest cars, and exotic vacations...and a part of me wonders if we weren't better off before.

I sigh and flush, feeling guilty, as if I am betraying my parents with my thoughts. They are *baalei tzedakah*, upright people, respected in our community and worldwide. I am proud of them, really I am.

But...I miss them.

The phone rings loudly, and I jump. I grab it, hoping to hear my parents' reassuring voices on the other end.

"Hi, Atara," comes Yocheved's clear voice.

"Hi," I say, trying to maintain a perky tone. I don't want my friends to realize how lonely I am.

Yocheved lapses into a discussion about something that happened during that day's English class. I am hardly paying attention. Her words just don't interest me at the moment.

"...drama re-tryouts," Yocheved is saying. There is a moment of silence, and then I hear her ask, in a slightly exasperated tone, "Atara, are you there?"

"Yes," I say sheepishly. "Sorry. What were you saying?"

"I was just asking you what happened during recess today."

"Oh." I think for a moment, wondering what to say. I haven't yet hashed out that morning's re-tryouts with my friends. There isn't much to say, after all. I think back to that half hour in the library. It was nerve-wracking, true, but it was also good, in an intangible kind of way. I read a few lines with Brachie Bodner, and I think it went well.

But does that mean the lead role has already been assigned to someone else, and the heads were trying to figure out the rest of the cast list? Or were they using today's re-tryouts to figure who would garner the main role? The insecurity of it all is eating me up, and I don't want to go there.

"It was okay," is all I say, summing up the experience in three short words. Then I steer the conversation in another direction, and Yocheved innocently follows my lead. I exhale, relieved, and allow my mind to wander once again while she prattles on.

Next week — Monday during recess — we will find out who

landed the starring role. I can already see my name in big, bold letters next to the line that says "Gracia."

I half-close my eyes and revel in the image. It's not time for bed yet — but I am already dreaming.

CHAPTER 8

Brachie

THERE IS SOMETHING about Friday afternoons, and it's not only the fact that Shabbos is coming in just a few hours.

Every week, when I exit the doors of Bais Breindel, I feel liberated, freed, as if I could sprout wings and fly. That is most certainly a cliché, but there's no other way to describe the lightness I feel as I leave school a few blocks behind me.

I am going home, where, for the next two days, I can be *me*, Brachie Bodner. I will not be The Principal's Daughter; I will not have to put on a pretense of perfection or make sure to greet everyone with a calm, confident smile.

I am smiling as I near my house and turn up the walkway. The smile quickly disappears, though, as soon as I notice a familiar green minivan parked outside my house, a few inches from the curb.

"Hi, Brachie!" I can hear Chevy's voice before I see her. I half turn, to see her emerging from the back of her car, the baby in her arms.

"Hi," I say, trying to sound enthusiastic.

So much for heading home to some peace and quiet. The commotion is already starting.

"Why are you here so early, Chevy?" I ask, trying not to sound accusatory.

Chevy laughs lightly as she motions to her husband which suitcases to bring in first. I blanch as Ari hauls in two enormous duffel bags. Are they planning to stay the week?

"Go hold Tante Brachie's hands," Chevy tells her two oldest children. Shimmy and Sima are instantly by my side, their sticky hands pressed into mine. They are cute, my niece and nephew, and I smile at them. Their mother, though, is another story.

"Why'd you come so early?" I ask again.

Chevy yawns. "Well, the baby kept me up all night, and I'm soo exhausted. And..."

"You want me to watch the kids for you." My voice is flat.

I'm not surprised that Chevy misses the tension in my tone. "You're the best, Brachie!" she says. She looks at her children. "Who thinks Tante Brachie is the best?"

She sounds like she's leading a color war cheer, and I grimace. I walk with my niece and nephew toward my house, my mouth set in a thin line. "I have to help Ima get ready for Shabbos," I say, without looking back.

"You know Ima," Chevy says flippantly. "She's always finished by now."

I sigh, knowing that Chevy is right about that. My ever-efficient mother cooks until late Thursday night and then wakes up early on Friday morning to take care of the last-minute touches and food preparation. When we come home from school on Erev Shabbos, the house is basically ready.

"Does Ima know you're coming so early?" I ask.

I can almost see Chevy shrug, though I'm not looking at her. "What's the big deal, Brachie? You know Ima couldn't care less when we come! But yes, I did give her a warning." She laughs, but I am not amused.

I step through the front door and see Chevy's suitcases cluttering the hallway. I know that soon her stuff will be sprawled all over the house, a hodgepodge of things infringing on the perfect order of our rooms. And who will be expected to help her get it all back together again?

I grit my teeth and try to escape upstairs, to my immaculate room.

"Hi, Brachie," my mother says, looking like she's enjoying all the commotion already. "Hi, kids. How are you, Chevy?" She squeezes Shimmy and Sima tightly and takes the baby from Chevy's arms.

"Hi," I say, taking a step in the direction of the stairs.

"One second," my mother says. "Brachie, can you help make up the beds for the kids in your room?"

I swallow. "*My* room?"

"Yes," my mother replies while cooing to the baby. "I forgot to ask you if you minded having some company over Shabbos. Since Shifra and Chaim are also coming, we're short on space."

"Um…" What should I say? What *is* there to say? My mother is asking me, but it's not like I have much of a choice. She *had* mentioned to me the other day that both Chevy and Shifra were visiting for Shabbos this week, but I just hadn't thought about what that would mean in terms of my own personal space being invaded... I guess I should have realized that this was coming. "Okay," I say in a small voice.

I am already feeling cornered and cluttered. As I head upstairs, I try to recapture the headiness I was feeling just minutes ago... but the feeling has vanished, and I know I won't be able to experience it again, at least not on this Shabbos.

Atara

DADDY AND MOMMY are coming home!

I can hear the birds twittering as I walk home from school, and it seems to me that they are echoing the singing in my heart. In fact, the whole world is sunnier, brighter, on this not-so-ordinary Friday afternoon.

I wave to Yocheved and Malkie as they turn down their block, and I continue on to my own. I barely notice the large houses I pass on the way. I am looking out only for my own — an enormous red-brick edifice set back from the street.

My legs bring me to it faster than usual, and I am fairly running up the elegant walk, not caring in the least bit that this does not at all befit my status as a mature high school student.

I press the doorbell and am buzzed in.

"Hi!" I cry as I step into the spacious foyer. To my disappointment, I see only Janet, who is brandishing a rag over a gold-framed mirror.

"Where are my parents?" I ask her, the heady anticipation I'd been feeling dissipating along with the mist coming from

Janet's spray bottle.

"Upstairs," Janet replies, rubbing the mirror with measured strokes. Within minutes the mirror is gleaming, but the same cannot be said of the way I'm feeling. I head upstairs, my feet suddenly heavy.

I can hear noise coming from the girls' room, and I tread down the hall. Esti, Elisheva, and Miri share an enormous room decorated in light shades of pink and ebony. Right now, their patterned carpet is strewn with boxes and bags.

Gifts. From my parents.

I burst into my sisters' room. "Shev?" I say to my sister, who is busy looking through a kaleidoscope covered with foreign words. "Where are Daddy and Mommy?"

Elisheva shrugs, too busy to look at me.

"Esti? Miri?"

It's no use. My little sisters are absorbed in their fancy new dolls, no doubt the best Europe has to offer.

I leave their room and head toward my own. I wonder if my parents have gone to take naps. I wonder —

"Atara!"

I look up to see my mother heading toward me, her arms outstretched. I fall into them, relief washing over me.

"I was looking for you," I say, then bite my tongue. I sound like I'm around the same age as my little sisters.

"I've been trying to unpack and get organized," my mother tells me. "I'm so tired, I lost track of when you'd be coming home." She looks at her watch and sighs. "It's hard to believe that Shabbos is in just a few hours."

That's the least of her concerns, and I know it. With Janet

around to take care of the cleaning and dish-washing, and Tziri Cohen's mother to send over whatever we don't already have in the freezer — and, knowing her, lots more besides that — we're all set. Erev Shabbos in our house is calm and predictable, even when my parents have just come home from across the Atlantic Ocean.

"So," my mother says, giving me a weary smile, "how was your week?"

I hesitate. Does she want the whole truth — that it was lonely and long? Or should I gloss over the stark details with some generic fluff?

"It was okay," I say, choosing the second option.

My mother looks relieved, and I say nothing.

Mommy, I want to tell her, *it was hard. It was hard not to have parents around; hard to be in charge of the little kids when they missed you; hard to have no mother to talk to... And it's even harder when I know this is probably going to happen again soon.*

Instead I say, "Where's Daddy?"

"Daddy actually fell asleep," my mother says. "He was trying to stay up so he could see you, but he couldn't keep his eyes open. I'll tell him you're home as soon as he wakes up."

I nod. My poor parents must be so jet-lagged and tired from their trip.

My mother walks with me toward my room, her arm around my shoulders. "I left presents on your desk," she tells me excitedly. "I think you're really going to like them."

I smile. Which girl wouldn't be thrilled at the thought of receiving glamorous gifts, selected from the high-class boutiques of Europe?

But as my mother's cell phone shrills and I hear her tell me, "One minute," my heart sinks. Oh, what I wouldn't give to have my parents' attention all to myself!

But I know that that's a silly thought. I'm a big girl, and my parents are busy people. I banish the notion from my mind just as quickly as it enters.

My mother hangs up after a hurried conversation. "That was Tami Roth," she tells me. "We're going to start planning for the Chinese auction next week."

"How nice," I say dismally, feeling that this nugget of news is anything but nice. My mother has chaired Chinese auctions to benefit Tikvah V'Yeshuah for three years already, and those long months she spends working on them stick out in my mind as a blur of hectic, crazy weeks when my mother is noticeably absent from our day-to-day lives.

"I can't wait for you to see the gifts I picked out," my mother says as we turn into my room. "You're going to love them."

But it's too late. The anticipation I felt just moments before has fizzled away.

CHAPTER 9

Brachie

"So, Brachie," Shifra says as she leans back into the couch, "how's school going?"

It's only twenty minutes after candle-lighting, and I just want to relax. Talking about school will most definitely not help me do that.

"*Baruch Hashem*," is all I say, half-closing my eyes. This afternoon was hectic and chaotic, and I am *tired*.

"Are you getting ready for production yet?" Chevy asks.

"They just broke it out," I say shortly. Of all my sisters, Chevy is the one who rubs me the wrong way. Maybe it's because she expects me to be her children's nanny whenever she comes to our house, or maybe it's because her easygoing, effervescent personality is so very different from my own. Whatever it is, I don't look forward to her family's visits.

Shifra gives a rapturous sigh. "Production," she whispers,

as if the very word evokes memories too wondrous to contain within those three syllables.

My gaze flits to Shifra, the sister closest to me in age. Shifra was in dance every year for production, and then she went on to head dance when she was in twelfth grade. I've always envied her effortless grace, the way she executes complicated steps with dainty precision.

"Production was fun," Chevy agrees, a smile playing on her lips. "Ima, what play is the school putting on this year?"

I am annoyed that Chevy is including my mother in this conversation. I wish that just this once, I could discuss something school-related without bringing my mother into it.

My mother looks up from the couch, where she's reading a book to Sima and Shimmy.

"Brachie can tell you," she says, and then continues reading aloud right from where she left off.

I'm grateful. "It's based on the book *With Hearts of Fire*," I tell my sisters.

"Ooh, that's a great story," Chevy says. "What did you try out for?"

"Drama," I answer quietly.

Chevy wrinkles her nose. "Weren't you in ensemble last year?"

I nod but don't say anything.

"So you don't want to be in ensemble again?" Chevy persists.

I am growing annoyed. Thankfully, Shifra tells Chevy just then, "Brachie is a great actress." From the mirthful look in her eyes, I can tell she's remembering a skit the two of us put on one Adar that had our family in stitches. We exchange grins.

"Usually girls like to be in the same group year after year,"

Chevy says. "I mean, how are the drama heads supposed to know you can act if you weren't in drama last year?"

"That's what tryouts are for." There is an edge to my voice.

"Girls change their minds all the time," Shifra cuts in. "Remember my friend Aidel? She has a beautiful voice, but she's also a great dancer. So after being in choir for two years, she decided she really wanted to be in dance for a change — and she switched."

Chevy shakes her head, her dark-brown *sheitel* swishing slightly. "I don't know," she says. "I think it's important to prove yourself in something."

I frown. Chevy's words have lodged more doubts in my mind. If it weren't enough that I'm worried about whether my status as Mrs. Bodner's daughter will work against me, I now need to fret over my lack of participation in drama last year. What if the heads somehow find out why I didn't get into drama then? What if they think I'm prone to stage fright or nervous attacks?

I try to reassure myself that the fact that I was called to try out again is a good sign, and especially the fact that I did a good job at the re-tryouts, too.

But then again, the other girls in the room were also called for re-tryouts, and they also performed great then…

"You don't want a big part, right?" Chevy continues relentlessly. She takes a break to coo at her baby. "Anyway, the big parts usually go to the older girls, girls in twelfth grade or maybe eleventh."

I sigh and sink deeper into the couch. I don't want to spend Shabbos worrying. I tell myself that we'll find out soon enough on Monday who landed which role, and that it's out of my hands anyway.

But I can't help casting a withering glance in Chevy's direction. Why, oh, why, did she have to come this Shabbos?

Atara

"Good Shabbos!"

My father walks through the front door, somehow looking both ebullient and exhausted. My sisters run toward him, their Shabbos shoes clacking against the shining marble floor.

"Wait!" My father laughs. "Let me take off my coat first."

I smile from my perch on the couch in the den. This is a Friday night ritual in my house, and right now a sign that things are more or less back to normal.

My mother stands up, stifling a yawn. She nods to Janet, who is bustling around the kitchen. Within moments, the sparkling wine and grape juice decanters are placed on the table, along with a hot challah from the oven. I lie lazily against the smooth leather cushion, wishing I could relax for another few minutes, but then force myself to stand up. I know my parents are tired and would like to make this an early night.

My father takes his place at the head of the table. I smile as my sisters join in for *"Shalom Aleichem,"* their high-pitched voices soaring above my father's bass.

It's a typical Shabbos in the Gold house, and I am savoring the ordinariness of it. Just last week, I sat in this stiff, high-backed chair, nervously anticipating my parents' trip. And now it is over, and they are home again. *Baruch Hashem.*

It's time for Kiddush, and we all rise in unison. I look around the table at my little sisters, in their matching burgundy robes and huge bows adding the perfect touch to their blonde heads. We are a perfect-looking family, I think to myself.

The swish of the faucet being turned on in the kitchen competes with my father's voice as he holds his exquisite silver Kiddush cup. I frown, annoyed. Why does Janet have to choose just this moment to wash her hands?

A few minutes later, peace reigns again as we bite into the warm challah.

"Tell us about Italy!" Miri begs.

My father smiles. "Well…"

"Didn't you go to Paris?" Esti asks, confused.

I bite back a grin. The names of exotic cities swirl around our house, confusing my little sisters — and sometimes even me.

"Actually, I'm going there in another couple of weeks," my father says, looking fondly at Esti.

"You are?" I blurt out.

My father looks at me, surprised. "Yes, I have to take care of some business there."

You're leaving us again? I think, but say nothing.

Elisheva glances at my mother. "Are you also going?" she asks.

My mother shakes her head. "No, I've had enough traveling for a while," she says, smiling. "Though it was nice!"

I am relieved, but then remember how her work on the Chinese auction is going to start soon. I sit back in my seat, deflated.

My sisters are chatting, asking lively questions and keeping my parents busy. I suddenly have no desire to take part in their conversation.

I finger the thick links of the bracelet my parents bought for me. It's *the* latest in fashion, and I know my friends will go crazy over it. But right now, none of that matters. I don't need this bracelet, nor the stunning stud earrings sparkling in my earlobes. All I want is the knowledge that in ten days' time, I will have both of my parents here, in this house, focused on me and my sisters.

As I touch the cold metal glistening on my wrist, I am aware that all of the gifts in the world could never fill the void I feel right now.

Brachie

"Here, Chevy!" I practically throw Sima and Shimmy's pajamas into my sister's hands. I am itching to get their stuff out of my room and reclaim my privacy.

"What're you doing?" Chevy asks me.

"I'm helping you clean up," I inform her.

"We're not leaving yet," Chevy says. "We're staying over tonight, too."

I stare at her. "You are?"

"Yeah," Chevy says flippantly. "Ima doesn't mind, and it's easier for me to just put the kids to sleep here than to have them fall asleep in the car, only to wake up just when we get home." She rolls her eyes dramatically.

I place my hands on my hips, feeling most unsympathetic toward my sister's plight. "Well," I say, "Shifra and Chaim are leaving tonight. Aren't they?" Unless *everyone* decided to stay over this Motza'ei Shabbos without telling me?

Chevy smiles at her baby, then looks up at me. "Yeah, they're leaving soon."

"So we'll move Sima and Shimmy into their room," I finish triumphantly.

Chevy shakes her head. "It's too much work," she says. "It's not fair to Ima."

I glare at her, my mouth hanging open. There is so much I want to say. What about the fact that I want — that I *need* — my room back to myself? What about all the work Chevy keeps me busy with over Shabbos — picking up after her kids, cleaning their chocolate-smeared hands and mouths, finding their sippy cups...

Instead I say, "It's okay. I'll move the crib and mattress myself. Ima won't have to do a thing."

Chevy doesn't even give my words more than a second's worth of attention. "Nah," she says. "It's too hard on the kids to shuffle them around. They already slept in your room last night, so it'll be easier for them to fall asleep there tonight."

My mouth is opening and closing, and through my haze of anger, I'm aware that I resemble the goldfish my brothers owned once upon a time. But at the moment, I don't care.

"Ima," I say, when my mother enters the kitchen, "I don't want to sleep with Sima and Shimmy tonight."

My mother looks at me, then over at Chevy, who is spooning mashed banana into her baby's mouth. "I don't see why we can't move them to a different room," she says.

Chevy shakes her head again, not even bothering to look up.

"It's too hard," she says. The baby reaches out for the spoon, and some banana flies right onto my sister's velour robe. She grimaces.

"Too hard for who?" I sputter. My mother is shaking her head warningly at me, but I plow right ahead. "Tomorrow is Sunday, for your information, and I don't want to be woken up at six o'clock in the morning by your kids!"

Chevy pouts as she swipes at the banana with a napkin. "But I need help in the morning," she says. "Ari is going to the early *minyan*, and the baby keeps me up all night."

That does it. "I am not your babysitter!" I shriek, the words spewing out of my mouth before I can catch them. "I watched your kids the entire Shabbos — and the whole Friday, too! Enough is enough!"

The baby starts to cry. I can see everyone staring at me through the red cloud of fury that is enveloping me right now. Chevy's eyes are wide, filled with shock and hurt.

Let them stare at me! I think. *I don't care.*

I run upstairs and storm into my room. Within minutes, the crib and mattress are set up in the spare bedroom that Shifra has just vacated, alongside a duffel bag filled with Sima and Shimmy's clothes.

I look around, satisfied, before heading back into my own room and locking the door behind me.

Atara

"WHY DON'T YOU invite Yocheved over?" my mother suggests. "Or how about Malkie or Chana Rochel?"

CURTAIN CALL • 75

I shake my head. I'm in no mood to have friends over. I stretch my legs, trying to get into a more comfortable position on the couch. I can hear Janet bustling around in the kitchen, setting up for an elaborate *melaveh malkah*.

Milchig melaveh malkahs are a Gold family tradition, and I'm loath to give up private time with my parents to spend it with a friend.

"You've been so quiet over Shabbos," my mother says, looking concerned. "Are you feeling okay?"

I nod, secretly enjoying the attention. But then the phone rings, and the moment is gone.

"Hello?" my mother says. "Oh, hi, Shoshana! How are you?"

She tucks the phone under her chin and sits down on an armchair, settling into a leisurely conversation. I sigh and stare at the oversized portrait of myself that is hanging on the wall. I was five when the picture was taken, and my dark-blue eyes are brimming with happiness. I gaze longingly at the carefree smile of the Atara of long ago, wishing I could recapture just a tiny bit of that pure joy.

How simple life was when I was little! My little sisters are growing up so differently than I did. I wonder if a photographer would be able to catch that same exquisite happiness on their faces.

They *are* happy, though, my sunny, sparkling sisters. They have been raised in this beautiful home, with its porcelain dolls and shelves stuffed with games. They have everything money can acquire for them, and they don't know what they're missing.

But I do.

"I'll call you back later, Shoshana," my mother says, smiling. "The Cohens should be here any minute for *melaveh malkah*."

Whatever she says after that is lost on me. I hadn't realized we were having guests tonight. My parents enjoy hosting, it's true, but I was not expecting to share them this evening.

No doubt they want to regale the Cohens with details of their trip. I stand up slowly from the couch, stretching my cramped muscles. My mother is issuing last-minute instructions to Janet, and she does not notice my exit.

I head up the winding staircase situated right off the den, my fingers trailing lightly on the smooth banister. Then I go into my room and gently close the door behind me.

CHAPTER 10

Brachie

The only thing I want to do right now is: escape.

Chevy's accusing eyes are still following me around the house this morning, and I've had enough. I know my mother wants to talk about what happened last night, but she's so busy tending to Chevy's kids that she hasn't had a chance. It's hard to have a serious conversation between diapers and breakfast and tantrums.

I call Dassi and ask her if she'd like my company this morning. She's surprised but grateful, and I'm happy to be of service. Dassi never expects anything of me. If I help her, she thanks me, and if I stay on the sidelines, that's fine, too. Maybe that's why I look up to my oldest sister so much.

"Ima," I say, trying to talk over the din Shimmy is creating. He wants a chocolate bar for a snack, and Chevy isn't backing down from her refusal.

My mother looks at me, a question in her eyes. I suddenly feel bad for abandoning her to this hullabaloo, but I need to get away.

"Do you mind if I go to Dassi?" I ask hesitantly.

My mother gazes at me, understanding in her eyes. "Go ahead," she tells me gently.

A few minutes later, I'm ready. I give Sima and Shimmy quick hugs and kiss the baby. "Bye!" I call over my shoulder. I haven't exchanged a word with Chevy all morning, and I'm not about to start now.

I exhale with relief as I step out into the bright sunshine. The world seems more promising now that I'm embracing it head-on. I walk for several minutes, enjoying the crisp breeze ruffling my ponytail, the sense of freedom that fills me like helium in a balloon.

I can see Dassi's complex looming ahead. Her building is filled with young families just like her own, and the lobby is cluttered with carriages and riding toys, doll strollers and bikes. I walk inside, sidestepping a scooter lying in my path.

The elevator door slides open a moment after I press the button, and I step inside with the familiarity of one who visits this building often.

I am soon striding down the fourth-floor hallway. I can see Dassi's door, slightly ajar.

"She's coming! She's coming!" someone yells excitedly.

I smile and quicken my pace. The door is flung open, and Zissy barrels into my arms.

"Hi!" I say, pushing her soft bangs out of her eyes.

I walk into the house to see Tova smiling shyly at me. At her side is a girl I've never seen before, staring at me with big eyes.

Dassi is struggling to dress Yechiel on the couch, but she looks up and smiles. "Hi, Brachie! How'd you know we were in desperate need of your company today?"

I laugh. Dassi has a way of cheering me up no matter what my mood might be.

"Do you want me to take over?" I ask as Yechiel wriggles out of her grasp.

Dassi laughs. "Think you'll have better luck than me? Sure, go ahead."

I deftly dress my little nephew. He's too confused by my presence to put up much of a fuss.

"Wow, Brachie," Dassi says with admiration. "You're really quick."

I smile. I'm rather like my mother — efficient, reliable, and organized. With her super laidback personality, Dassi is as different from the rest of us as an apple from a banana. But despite that, she makes everyone warm up to her immediately with her irresistible good cheer and sunny personality.

I move aside some clothes and packages of wipes — I try not to wonder why she has three of them open at the moment — and settle into her sagging couch. I feel relaxed in a way I can only feel at Dassi's house.

Yechiel toddles over to a closet and overturns two baskets filled with toys. Dassi sighs, then grins good-naturedly.

"Why don't you keep it locked?" I ask her.

Dassi shrugs. "There is a lock for it — somewhere." She motions toward the heaps of odds and ends scattered all over the floor. I can't help but grin, too.

"Tova, who's your friend?" I ask my niece.

Tova looks at her friend, and the two little girls giggle.

"That's Miri," Dassi says, smiling at them.

I take in Miri's perfectly-tailored dress and the headband that is the exact same shade as the deep-purple ruffles along her wrists and hem. I can't help but contrast that with Tova's dress, which is faded and in need of some ironing.

There's something so sweet, so innocent, about little kids, before they're old enough to judge each other based on externals. For a moment I wish I could travel back in time and be a little girl again, not passing judgment on others for superficial reasons and not feeling like I myself am under constant scrutiny. I sigh.

"What's wrong?" Dassi wants to know.

I want to confide in her so badly, to tell her about Shabbos and how Chevy treats me like the family maid. The words are about to tumble out of my mouth, but I bite them back. Instead, I discuss another topic that's burning in my mind.

"I'm so nervous," I tell my sister. "Tomorrow they're posting the cast list for the play."

Dassi nods understandably. "I remember those days," she says, her eyes half-closing nostalgically. "It's funny how we used to think production was everything in life."

I mull that over. Do I think production is everything? It's definitely occupying a nice chunk of my thoughts, but that doesn't mean it's my only priority, does it?

Dassi changes the topic before I have time to process my thoughts. "By the way, Brachie, is Ima feeling okay?" Her eyes squint the way they do when she's concerned about something.

Dassi's words bring up the unsettling questions flitting around my own head about Ima's recent, extreme tiredness.

"I...I don't know," I say thoughtfully. "I mean, she's been really tired lately, but she was okay on Shabbos, I think." I close my eyes, trying to remember. Shabbos had been so hectic that I hadn't noticed how often my mother slept or how she was feeling. "Why do you ask?"

Dassi shrugs. "Ima's been sounding kind of out of it when I call," she says. "But it's probably nothing. She works so hard and has so much on her head."

We both are silent, wrapped in troubling thoughts. Dassi finally turns to me with a smile. "I'm sure everything's fine, Brachie," Dassi says. "Ima's only human. Anyone with half her load would feel overwhelmed."

I nod, but the disturbing doubts continue to pursue me. Ima has been a powerhouse since my earliest memories. The image of my mother, rubbing her eyes after an unusually long afternoon nap, commenting on how weary she is, just isn't compatible with the mother I've grown up with.

"Anyway," Dassi says, changing the topic yet again, "you have to see the cutest new book my sister-in-law bought for the kids."

She heads toward the bookcase just as Yechiel manages to pull the tablecloth off the dining room table. Plates, picture albums, papers, and piles of other things I can't even identify fall to the floor.

"Oh, no!" Dassi exclaims, running toward the mess.

The doorbell rings, and she looks at me.

"Do you mind getting the door, Brachie? It's probably Miri's mother. She said she'd pick her up around now."

"Sure," I say. I pick my way through all the things littering the floor, wondering if Dassi is embarrassed that someone will observe her house in this state. I know I'd be mortified.

A moment later I *am* mortified, as I stare into the bemused eyes of the person standing at Dassi's doorstep. I want to moan, groan, run away, sink right underneath the piles of toys and clothes all over the worn carpet...but I don't have the luxury of doing any of those options.

Instead, I force myself to say hello to Atara Gold.

Atara

I AM STARING INTO Brachie Bodner's brown eyes, curiosity dimming my usual composure.

"Brachie, what are you doing here?" I blurt out.

She does not quite meet my eyes when she answers. "This is my sister's house."

"Your sister?" I look past Brachie into the little apartment. Things are strewn all over the place, and there's a woman wearing a black, slightly stretched-out snood sitting on the floor. "Oh, that's so funny!" I say. "I never put two and two together."

Is it my imagination, or is Brachie decidedly uncomfortable? I wonder about that. This home exudes such calmness and warmth. How many other mothers could sit there amid such a mess and still smile? Brachie's sister must be one of those amazing people you read about who can handle *anything*.

"You must be Miri's sister," Mrs. Fleishman says, extricating herself from the pile she's been putting together. "She's so cute — we really enjoyed her!"

"Thank you," I reply, reverting back to my gracious self. "We can't wait to have Tova over one day."

Brachie is standing there, looking back and forth from me to her sister as if she's watching a ping-pong game. And suddenly I realize: Brachie must be thinking about drama tryouts. We are two contestants now, in pursuit of the same gold medal, and at this point she views me as formidable competition.

I flinch. I don't want to focus on that during this chance meeting outside of school. I want to revel in the cozy atmosphere of this humble apartment, if only for the few minutes I am standing here.

"Dassi, where'd you put Miri's coat?" Brachie asks urgently.

"Check the hook on Tova and Zissy's door."

Brachie fairly sprints down the hall, no doubt eager to banish me from her sister's turf. I try to be understanding, but I'm hurt. There is life beyond production, isn't there?

"So, you're Mrs. Bodner's daughter," I comment to Brachie's sister.

She smiles, and her whole face lights up. "Lucky me," she says.

I laugh. I like Mrs. Fleishman already.

"How's my mother treating you?" she asks with a wink.

Brachie chooses that moment to appear with Miri's coat. Her mouth is stretched in a taut line, and she dresses Miri herself.

"I can do that," I say quickly.

"It's okay," Brachie tells me, pulling the ornate purple buttons through their hooks. "Bye, Miri," she says, as if shooing her away.

"Come again, Miri," Mrs. Fleishman calls. She prompts her daughter. "Tova, what do you say?"

"Thank you for coming," the little girl says automatically. She's cute, and I smile at her.

Then Brachie is at the door, swinging it closed.

"Nice seeing you, Atara," she says.

I can take a hint. "You, too," I say stiffly, and turn to leave, holding my sister's hand tightly.

Miri is chattering while we take the elevator down to the lobby, and then when we walk outside to the parking lot, but I'm hardly listening. My mother's gleaming SUV is hovering near the front of the lot, and I help Miri climb inside.

"Did you have a nice time, Miri?" my mother asks, turning around in her seat to smile at my little sister.

Miri nods and giggles. "Tova's house is so much fun!"

"Why?" Esti and Elisheva demand to know.

Miri launches into a blow-by-blow account of how she and Tova colored, and then did a project with stickers, and how they had potato chips for snack.

I tune her out and stare out the window as the scenery passes me by. I am thinking of Mrs. Fleishman, and how relaxed and inviting she is. My parents host guests all the time, whether it's for an elegant Shabbos meal or stately parlor meeting. But there was something there, in that small apartment strewn with toys and what-not — something so natural and warm and welcoming...

Then I remember Brachie, and her cold reception.

I flinch. I've always admired Brachie, and it's not just because she's Mrs. Bodner's daughter. I wonder why she was so stiff toward me, if she really was only thinking about drama. But if it wasn't that, then what could it be?

CURTAIN CALL • 85

"Who wants pizza?" my mother says as the car cruises down Spruce Street.

"Me!" my sisters chorus.

My mind flits back to Mrs. Fleishman. I wonder whether *she* ever takes her kids out for pizza. And the next second I wonder why I even care.

CHAPTER 11

Brachie

I'LL NEVER BE ABLE to look Atara Gold in the face again.

My head is down as I walk to school Monday morning, reliving yesterday's humiliation. I'm so upset — and I don't even know at whom!

That makes everything so much more confusing. Am I angry at Dassi, my friendly, fun-loving big sister? I think of the mess that characterizes her home, and how it never really bothered me before. Her house is like her personality — inviting and warm, effusive and joyful.

Dassi's positive attributes far outweigh her lack of organization — but for Atara Gold to witness the Fleishman home at its worst! The very thought sends my stomach catapulting to my knees all over again.

How could Dassi do this to me? I wonder, while knowing that my reasoning at the moment is far from logical. But I'm too focused on one thing: what is Atara *thinking*?

Is she going to tell her clique — all of them perfectly put-together, like her — just how scatterbrained Mrs. Bodner's daughter is? Is she laughing at me? Wondering how I can possibly share the same genetic pool as Dassi? Or...maybe she thinks I'm just as disorganized in the privacy of my own home? That the principal's home is just as flying and frenzied as her oldest daughter's?

I shudder and continue to plod on. The only thing keeping me going is the knowledge that today, during recess, the cast list for this year's play will be posted on the bulletin board, in all its black-and-white glory. I am itching, aching, to know what role — if any — I am assigned.

I think longingly of how a starring role would show everyone just how capable Brachie Bodner is. In one sweeping night, I will prove myself to my classmates, to my sisters, to everyone who ever thought of me as merely The Principal's Daughter.

And most important, I will prove myself...to myself.

If only...

Atara

IF ONLY recess would be one minute away instead of forty-three minutes and twenty-seven seconds.

Morah Leibman has only been talking for two minutes, but there's no way I can see myself getting through this whole class. I wonder if the bulletin board allotted for production announcements is already carrying The Paper, the one that will delineate which girls landed which roles.

I shiver, but not because I'm cold. I'm filled with icy apprehension, mixed with intense curiosity and laced with excitement. If I land the part of the righteous Gracia, I will be an instant star in this school — in the whole community, in fact.

My gaze flits nervously around the room. Most girls are busy penning notes as quickly as they can; no one talks faster than our *parshah* teacher. My own hands are way too jittery to even hold a pen; I'll catch up on the notes later, with the aid of Malkie's meticulous notebook.

I catch Yocheved's eye, and she grins. I give her a lukewarm smile in return. I peek at my watch, noting that only two minutes and eighteen more seconds have passed, before making another effort to bestow my attention on the teacher.

I force myself to look forward, to the front of the classroom, when my eyes fall upon a girl, her slight form hunched over her notebook. She is writing furiously, her brown ponytail swaying gently with the movement of her arm.

Brachie Bodner.

I marvel at her composure. How can she take notes as if her life depends on it when, in another forty minutes, the bell will blare, announcing that it's time to dash downstairs and read the paper we've waited for with bated breath?

I wish I could ask her how she can compartmentalize her feelings so easily. But then I remember our encounter yesterday, how Brachie was decidedly so unhappy to see me — and I know that I won't be asking Brachie this question, or any other questions, for that matter. Because obviously Brachie Bodner is not too fond of yours truly.

Brachie

NEVER HAS A CLASS PASSED BY with such agonizing slowness.

I flex my cramped hand, which hasn't stopped writing the entire time Morah Leibman was speaking. Throwing myself into this *parshah* class helped the time pass somewhat — but it still seemed to creep by. I take another peek at my watch, noting with both satisfaction and apprehension that the minute hand has almost neared its goal.

Morah Leibman pauses to take a breath, and I look at her hopefully. Maybe she'll dismiss us a few minutes early today. Maybe —

"Now, girls," she says, plowing right into another thought.

I try not to let the disappointment show on my face. I can hear faint exhales of frustration from those around me, but I know the sheer desperation I feel far surpasses whatever impatience my classmates might be feeling, wanting to get recess started already.

Morah Leibman is just wrapping things up when the bell rings, loudly and clearly. I jump in my seat, then look around, embarrassed. My jerky behavior is most unbefitting of The Principal's Daughter.

Morah Leibman continues to talk, and I stay respectfully in my seat, along with my classmates. Finally, after a few excruciating minutes — which seem to feel more like a few days — Morah Leibman exits the room.

I suddenly can't move. I am overcome by anxiety. What if I didn't get a leading role? What if I didn't get *any* part? What if —?

"Are you going downstairs?"

I look up to see Devora standing over me. "Don't you want to see the cast list?" she asks.

I nod, but my legs feel like heavy rubber, and I don't think I can move them.

"Nervous?" Devora gives me an understanding smile. Oddly, that gives me the strength I need to get out of my seat.

I feel as if I have temporarily entered another world. Around me, girls are talking, eating, studying, laughing. I view them as if from a murky distance. Their voices sound far away, echoing slightly in my ears.

I follow Devora automatically, not really paying attention to where I'm going. Each step brings me closer to the cast list, and I can't decide if I should keep going or run back to the safety of oblivion that my classroom offers.

There is a crowd of girls pressed around the bulletin board as we exit the stairwell, and I feel deflated and frightened. Now that I am only a mere few feet away from the cast list, I need to see it and know what it says *now*.

"Come," Devora says, navigating through the crowd. She is tall and broad, and it's easier for her to push her way in. I am right behind her, mumbling, "Excuse me" and, "I'm sorry" as I bump into girls, until finally we are close enough to the cast list to be able to read it.

My heart is thumping wildly, my head is pounding, and my fingers are trembling.

"Gracia," I read, not even aware that I'm whispering the word aloud. I follow the line to the column right beside it, the one labeled "Cast," and see the name "Nechama Korn."

Disappointment washes over me, wave after wave of cold frustration. How I wanted that role so badly!

But maybe I was assigned another leading role?

"Francesca," I read next. Who will be Gracia's timid sister and revel in loads of time in the limelight as well? "Michal Rabinowitz," I murmur, the name tasting bitter to me.

Where is my name? Oh, where is my name? I skim the lines anxiously. And then I see it.

A bit further down the list, beside "Maria, servant one," appears "Brachie Bodner" in flat, dark letters.

Though girls are pressing in on me from all sides, I can't move. Despair fills me from head to toe so I can hardly breathe.

"Lucky you," I hear Devora say.

Her voice is fuzzy, as if she's speaking to me long-distance. *Is she talking to me? Why would she be telling me that I'm lucky?*

I force myself to look at Devora, to think beyond my own disappointment. "Did you get a part?" I ask her.

She nods too quickly, and I can see disappointment filling her eyes. "I'm going to be one of the stablemen," she says.

"Oh," is all I can reply. Poor Devora, who has only about two lines to say in the entire play. And poor me.

"You have a good part," Devora tells me. "There's an entire scene with just Maria and Juanita. And you'll get to appear throughout the play."

It's true, and I know it. It *is* a pretty decent role — but it's not the leading one.

I try to paste a smile on my face, if only so as not to hurt Devora. How can I carry on about the role I was assigned when hers is so much worse?

For one frenzied moment, I toy with the idea of running to my mother's office to indulge in a good cry. The next second, I chuck the notion scornfully. All I need is for one person to see me there, and I'll be branded forever as Crybaby Brachie, who runs to her mother the principal the minute things don't go her way.

I toss my head, as if telling all those would-be gossipers that The Principal's Daughter is quite in control of her emotions, thank you very much.

And then I see her, and I want to run away all over again. The mortification of yesterday's encounter is still too fresh, even with today's disappointment slapping me in the face.

Looking warily at me, her green eyes glistening slightly, is Atara Gold.

Atara

I STARE AT THE LIST, colors blurring before my eyes until I can see nothing besides bright blobs. There is the red of fury, the black of despair, the brown of disappointment, mingling with the white of the bright lights above and the beige of the speckled walls that form a backdrop to this traitorous bulletin board.

I shake my head and blink rapidly, as if there is just a minor problem with my eyesight and in a moment I will see my name where it belongs — right next to "Gracia."

Instead, to my intense frustration, it's right where I saw it the first time, next to "Juanita, servant two." I want to scream, shake someone, rip down the list, run away...but instead I stand there, trembling silently, squeezing my hands so tightly that my knuckles are whiter than chalk. I bite my lip until I can taste blood on my tongue, and still I don't move. I don't know how I'll get over this blow, but I do know one thing: I will not let on to anyone just how deep my disappointment runs.

I scan the cast list from the beginning, curious to see who landed which parts. I skip over the lines reading "Gracia" and "Francesca" — they're just too painful. As I skim the list, my eyes widen in shock. Of all the girls in the entire cast, the one who appears on stage with me throughout the play is… Brachie Bodner.

If I am disappointed to be cast as Juanita, I am absolutely horrified to have to work so closely with Brachie. For some reason, she just doesn't like me — that much was clear at her sister's house the day before.

Girls continue to jostle me as I stand still like a statue, tears welling up in my eyes. I finally turn around, so I can head dejectedly back upstairs to my classroom.

And that's when I see Brachie Bodner staring at me, a funny expression on her face.

CHAPTER 12

Brachie

"Hi, Brachie!"

I'm relieved to hear my mother's voice greet me at the end of this long, never-ending day. After the morning's aggravation and the sheer effort it took to sit through class after class, I almost can't believe that I'm actually standing in our familiar front hallway now.

"Hi, Ima," I say as I hang up my coat.

"So?" my mother says as she comes out of the kitchen. "That was a nice surprise, wasn't it?"

"Huh?" I stare at my mother, confused.

"The cast list," my mother explains, her eyes twinkling.

"Oh." My own eyes shutter. "I guess so."

My mother picks up on the flatness in my voice right away. "What's the matter, Brachie?" she asks. "Aren't you happy to get such a big role?"

"A big role?" I echo bitterly. "It doesn't seem like a big role to *me*."

My mother is taken aback. "I thought you'd be thrilled."

I gaze at her suspiciously, a niggling thought suddenly pricking at my brain. "Ima, did you make sure they gave me a part in the play?"

My mother shook her head. "I didn't get involved in the casting at all. The teachers and I do look over the list before it's finalized, to make sure we're okay with it, but I didn't say a word to the drama heads about you."

I'm relieved. But… "I wanted the leading role!" I blurt out. "I wanted to be Gracia."

My mother nods understandingly. "I'm sure all the girls were dreaming of being picked to play Gracia. It's only natural."

That makes me think. I'm not the only one walking around feeling like a deflated balloon, with sharp tears pricking at my eyes and a sour taste in my mouth. I sigh.

"I think you'll have a great time playing this role," my mother says. "And you'll see — in your own way, you'll make your role stand out. I know you're a great actress."

But if only everyone else knew it, too, I want to say. Instead, I keep my thoughts to myself. I don't want my mother to know about my insecurities, to know how hard it is for me to walk the tightrope of being her daughter. Although I have a suspicion that she knows all that anyway.

The phone rings, and we both turn to look at it.

"Do you mind getting that, Brachie?" my mother asks.

"Sure," I say, though I'm almost positive it won't be for me. Ever since I started high school, the phone calls for me have dwindled down to a handful spread over a long range of months. I can't blame my classmates, exactly. I also wouldn't be running to call the principal's house if there were other houses I could call instead.

I pick up the phone, feeling that familiar surge of loneliness. "Hello?"

"Hi, Brachie," comes a hesitant voice.

"Oh. Chevy," I say, my own voice just as lukewarm.

Neither of us say anything for a few long seconds.

"I'll go give the phone to Ima," I finally say, just as Chevy says, "So, did you get to see the cast list for drama?"

I sigh, not in the mood to go there.

"Yes," I reply tersely. "One minute, please. Ima?"

"Wait," Chevy says. "Did you get a part?"

"Yes," I say, my voice on edge. If this polite conversation is Chevy's peace offering to me, I can live without it.

"So, what are you?"

"One of the servants." *How fitting. Just like I'm one of your servants.* I head to the kitchen in search of my mother, eager to hand her the phone.

"Is it a big part?"

"Yes. No. I don't know."

"Huh?" Chevy laughs. "Either it is or it isn't. But I was right, wasn't I? The heads wouldn't want to give a big part to someone who wasn't in drama before."

I growl at the phone. I know she's wrong. Atara Gold was in drama last year, and *her* part is the same size as mine.

So there, I think, but I don't bother rehashing the issue with my know-it-all sister. What's the point?

CURTAIN CALL • 97

"Ima," I call out, my voice dripping with artificial sugar, "Chevy's on the phone."

My mother looks at me for a moment before taking the phone. There's a strange expression in her eyes, but she says nothing.

"Hi, Chevy," she says into the phone. I turn away, feeling guilt and regret knot up my insides. Don't all parents want their children to get along? I try not to think about how my bickering with Chevy must be hurting my mother.

It's Chevy's fault, I tell myself self-righteously. *She's older, and she treats me like a shmatte.*

But it takes two to tangle, a soft voice whispers in my ear.

I absently take an apple from the fridge as my mother continues to talk to my sister. I'm only fifteen years old. Do I really have it within me to step back and make peace with my older sister?

I shake my head as I take a crisp, tangy bite. I don't know. I just don't know.

Atara

THE FIRST THING THAT STRIKES ME as I push open the heavy wooden door is the buzz of activity in the background. I don't see it right away, but it's a persistent drone hovering in the periphery of this grand house. I wonder what's going on.

"Mommy?" I call.

To my annoyance, Janet appears in the shining entranceway. "Your mom's in the basement," she tells me.

"Okay, thanks," I reply.

I run up the wide staircase just off the hallway to deposit my knapsack in my room, then come careening down again. I am about to fling open the door leading to the basement when my mother comes upstairs, a sleek blonde *sheitel* on her head.

"Hi, Atara." She gives me a wave.

"Hi. What's going on?" I ask her.

"We're hosting a speech tonight downstairs," my mother says. "I just wanted to make sure the chairs were being set up properly — there are a few people downstairs now taking care of it."

"Oh," I say. Our basement is huge — it runs along the entire length of our house — and we often host speeches and other community events down there.

"How was school?" my mother asks.

"Okay," I say, wincing. "They posted the cast list today."

"Really!" my mother says, her eyes gleaming. "And which part did my drama queen get?"

I flinch and feel my cheeks flush. "Um...not such a great one. I'm one of the servant girls who spies on the Jewish family and reports on them to the Inquisition."

"That sounds interesting," my mother says. "I'm sure you'll do a great job with it."

I shrug.

"You seem upset, Atara," my mother says.

I shrug again. There are no words that can express how upset I really am.

"I guess...I don't know." I fumble around for something to say, but instead give a feeble laugh. "I wouldn't have minded getting the lead role."

CURTAIN CALL • 99

My mother puts her arm around my shoulder. "I'm sure you wouldn't have, Tari," she says. "But you'll steal the spotlight in your own way."

I blink back tears, feeling like a little girl again.

"Not always is it the leading actress who shines," my mother tells me. "Even someone with one line can make her part stand out so everyone remembers her."

I shake my head dismally. Right now I don't want to be comforted. The pain is too raw, too fresh.

"When do rehearsals start?" my mother asks, trying to distract me.

"Tomorrow," I whisper, swallowing hard.

My mother is about to say something when the phone rings. I can hear Janet answering it in the kitchen. A moment later, I can hear the flip-flap of her rubber-soled slippers as she heads in our direction.

"It's for Atara," Janet says, holding out the phone.

My mother takes it from her and presses "mute."

"Do you want to take the call, Atara?" she asks gently.

I sigh but hold out my hand for the phone. I wouldn't mind some chitchat to distract me at the moment.

"I'll be in the kitchen if you need me," my mother tells me as I climb the winding staircase.

"Thanks," I tell her, as I click the "mute" button again. "Hello?"

"Hi, Atara," comes Chana Rochel's cheerful voice. "What's doing?"

"Since I last saw you forty-five minutes ago? Nothing." My head is throbbing, and I hope she doesn't catch my lackluster tone.

Chana Rochel giggles. "You know what I'm calling about," she says. "About drama…"

I am instantly on guard. "What about it?"

"Malkie said her sister said you got one of the best parts in the play," Chana Rochel says.

"Oh, did she?" I try to maintain a neutral tone, but my skepticism can't help making its presence known.

"Why, you don't think so?" Chana Rochel is genuinely astonished.

I sigh. I don't even know why I'm bothering to discuss it. The whole day I've been receiving congratulations from my classmates, words that I don't even want to hear and certainly not to accept.

True, in the scheme of the whole play, my part is significant enough — but it's not the leading role. And that's not something I want to discuss with anyone, or expect them to understand. Unless they vied for the main role, sat through the tension of tryouts, and put their heart on the line in front of a roomful of girls, how can I expect them to understand how I feel?

Brachie Bodner went through the same thing.

The thought assaults me with both its simplicity and stark truth. I wonder if Brachie is just as devastated as I am, although it's highly unlikely. She's Mrs. Bodner's daughter, after all. I'm sure the *chinuch* she received from her home will keep her going despite any obstacles in her way. Besides, she wasn't even in drama last year. It's not like she would've come to tryouts with any great expectations.

I snort to myself. Even if Brachie *is* having a hard time, it's not like I'll ever come to having a heart-to-heart discussion about it with her — not in this lifetime, anyway. The thought of such a discussion taking place is so absurd that I laugh aloud, despite myself.

"Why are you laughing?" Chana Rochel asks, surprised.

"I'm not really," I reply, reverting right back to my melancholy self. "I was just thinking about something funny, except it's not really so funny…whatever. What were you saying?"

"I was just saying that everyone knew the main roles would go to eleventh or twelfth graders," Chana Rochel says. "It's like that every year."

"Oh, really?" My voice is icy. "I didn't realize that. I guess I figured that if you have talent, that counts for something."

"Of course it does," Chana Rochel says matter-of-factly. "And that's why you got the part that you did. But the main parts — they almost always go to the older girls. That's just the way things are."

Just the way things are.

I lie down on my bed, rumpling up the perfectly ironed bedspread. I don't want to admit it…it hurts to admit it…but Chana Rochel is right. I was just hoping that my incredible talent would blow the drama heads over and that I would get what I wanted so badly—even if that meant the heads having to go against "the way things are."

But obviously, that didn't happen.

An image of Brachie, standing by the bulletin board, a tortured expression on her own face, suddenly flits through my mind. And I wonder if she really does understand what I'm going through right now — and if she's going through it herself.

CHAPTER 13

Brachie

IT'S AMAZING TO THINK that this classroom is going to be a kind of home-away-from-home for me over the next couple of months.

In this room, we actresses will read our lines, eat cold suppers, share jokes and frustrations. At times we will sit on the sidelines, and at times bask in the rosy glow of attention; we will stumble and make mistakes, yet still persevere onward to our ultimate goal: putting on a perfect play.

I am both anxious and excited as I take a seat beside Devora. Zehava and Ricki look around the room, clearly energized tonight.

"Hi, everyone," Zehava speaks up. She glances at Ricki, and the two heads exchange a conspiratorial grin.

"We've worked really hard on the casting for this play," Zehava continues. "We tried to make everyone happy while giving you parts that we felt would be perfect for all of you."

She coughs and falters.

Ricki takes over. "We also tried really hard to cast you with other girls who we felt you had good chemistry with."

I am amused, to put it mildly. Never would I have thought that Atara Gold and I have good chemistry. That's a funny way to describe a relationship between two very different girls who don't even have a relationship!

"So, before we start," Ricki says, "we thought it would be a good idea for everyone to get a feel for the time period of the Inquisition. The heads of costume are already researching clothing from that time, so we can get as close to the real thing as possible."

I feel a tingle of excitement creep up my spine. They're really covering all bases!

"We're not sure how much you each know about the fifteenth century in Spain," Zehava says. "Even for those of you who already learned about it, you might not have been paying enough attention in class." She giggles, and a dimple flashes at each corner of her mouth. "So first of all, we really recommend that you all read *With Hearts of Fire*, if you haven't already. And even if you have read it, it might help you to read it again. That should really help you put the play in perspective."

Ricki looks at Zehava and takes over again. "We're going to tell you a bit about the time period of the Spanish Inquisition and what things were like for the Jews at that time. It'll help you, as actresses, feel for your characters." She looks down at the notebook in her hands and takes a deep breath.

I am tense as I sit in my seat. How will learning about the Inquisition help me empathize with the gentile character I'm supposed to portray? I wanted to show the world how I'd give anything to keep Torah and mitzvos, as Gracia — and instead, I'm supposed to pretend to lead an entire family to their gruesome deaths!

I wrap my arms around myself and shiver, though the classroom is heated.

"The Inquisition started in Rome but later spread to other countries — including Spain, where our play takes place," Ricki explains. "Its purpose was to weed out heresy and heretics — especially the Jews. Some Jews pretended to convert, and they were known as *conversos*. The Mendeles family in our play is one of those families."

Ricki looks up for a moment, and her eyes fall on Shani Baum, a tall eleventh grader. "Lots of *conversos* kept the mitzvos secretly but didn't tell their children they were Jewish until they were old enough to keep the secret, too. Shani's character, Miguel, finds out the truth just before his parents are arrested."

I squirm in my seat. I wouldn't have minded playing Miguel. I can see myself as the boy, reacting with revulsion as I find out that I belong to the religion I have learned to abhor. I envision myself following my "father" into our family's secret cellar, where a makeshift shul is set up...and recognizing other *conversos* whom I had always thought were devout Catholics.

"Lots of *conversos* were very important people in Spain," Ricki tells us. "The Mendeles family in our play is one of these well-known families. They even have an uncle who's a cardinal in the church. He's also a *converso*." Her gaze lingers on Mindy Blum. "That's Mindy's part."

CURTAIN CALL • 105

"Now," Zehava says, following Ricki's lead, "there were spies on the lookout everywhere, trying to pinpoint these heretics. Some of them even worked in the houses of the *conversos* themselves." She looks at me, and I can feel my cheeks flame. I lower my gaze self-consciously, hoping no one else notices.

"Brachie and Atara are going to be the maids who discover that the Mendeles family is keeping mitzvos secretly," Ricki tells everyone. "They're the ones who will plot the family's downfall. The parents will be arrested, and their children will be forced to decide what to do after that. But," she adds with a grin, "I'm getting ahead of myself."

"The tribunal," Zehava murmurs.

"Right," Ricki says. "I was just about to talk about that. When the tribunal accused Jews of heresy, they were sentenced to death by fire. That was called an *auto de fe*. Those were major events in Spain — and that's what the Mendeles parents have been sentenced to."

Zehava and Ricki confer quietly for a moment before turning to face us again.

"Any questions?" Ricki asks us.

The silence in the room stretches.

"Okay," Zehava speaks up. "Then that's enough history for now." She smiles as her gaze sweeps the room. "It's time to start our rehearsal."

Atara

I'M BORED. I can't help yawning through Zehava and Ricki's history lesson. I've read enough books about the Inquisition to teach the history myself. But finally, Zehava announces that it's time to start rehearsals, and I immediately perk up.

Despite not landing the part I'd wanted, I'm an actress by nature — and I want to act. That's why I sit back in my seat, deflated, when Ricki asks Nechama Korn and Michal Rabinowitz, the two starring eleventh graders, to come up to the front of the room. I don't see why the entire cast has to watch them wade through their lines, when we each have our own lines to get acquainted with.

"Tonight we'll go through Scene One, Act One, with everyone reading her lines aloud," Ricki tells us. "Zehava and I just want to get a picture of where you're all holding and which lines we need to spend more time on."

I grit my teeth. They need to get *another* picture of where we're holding? What was the point of both tryouts we endured just last week? How much more of a picture do they need?

I riffle through the papers of my script, hoping to see Juanita appear in this scene. I wouldn't want this night to be an absolute waste. Ah-ha! I smile, gratified, when I catch lots of lines with "my" name preceding them.

I hardly pay attention while Nechama and Michal assume the roles of the heroic Gracia and her sister Francesca. I don't want to focus on them. Instead, I busy myself perusing my own lines, so I don't have to imagine myself up there, standing tall and confident in the leading role.

Despite myself, I am swept up in the dramatic implications my role has to offer. It's quite different from any character I've ever played before. Juanita is devious and deceptive, cruel and conniving. In my mind, I picture myself holding the audience captive with my performance. The sheer authenticity of my acting will have them spellbound, terrified, swept back in time to the stately Mendeles estate. They will —

"Atara?"

"Huh?" I look around, confused. It seems like every pair of eyes in the room is trained on me, and I can feel my face turning crimson. "What?" I say to Ricki, who's looking strangely at me.

"I asked if you and Brachie could come up to the front of the room since I want you hanging around, 'snooping' on Don and Dona Mendeles, and being ready to say your own lines when they come up."

"Oh, sure," I say, trying to muster up the shreds of my self-assurance that have fallen to the wayside. How embarrassing to be caught daydreaming like this.

I head to the front of the room with measured footsteps and take my place beside Brachie. I don't look at her or at anyone else. I'm focused on only one thing: outdoing everyone else's performance to such a degree that it eclipses even the leading roles.

Brachie

THE LIVING ROOM LIGHTS are twinkling at me as I head up the walkway leading to my house. That means my mother is still up — or at least that she remembered to leave the house lit up for me. I am feeling pleased with myself as I open the door and step inside the front hall.

"Hello?" my mother calls from the living room. "I'm in here, Brachie."

"Hi," I answer as I hang up my coat. I make my way to the living room and perch myself on a cushioned rocking chair.

"How was your first rehearsal?" my mother asks from her seat on the couch.

"It wasn't bad," I say thoughtfully. It really wasn't. After looking around at the other girls in the room, and seeing how miniscule their roles were compared to mine, I couldn't feel that bad about being casted as Maria. Besides, I had to admit that Chevy was right. The biggest roles went to eleventh and twelfth graders. So all in all, I'm feeling a lot better about my role in the play.

I think fleetingly of Atara and then push her out of my mind. The two of us haven't exchanged so much as a glance earlier tonight, and I can't help but wonder how this is all going to play out.

"Everyone cooperated?" my mother asks with a wink.

I shrug uncomfortably. I don't like playing the part of the principal's spy, even though I know my mother is only making conversation. "Sure, why not?" is all I say in response.

"That's good," my mother says. She seems distracted, and I wonder why. She's still tired, it's true, but I assumed that as long as the status quo stayed static, everything was just fine. Was that faulty reasoning on my part?

"I'm leaving school early tomorrow," my mother tells me. She leans her head back on the floral-patterned couch and yawns.

"Oh?"

"I have a doctor's appointment." My mother issues the words calmly, matter-of-factly, but I am instantly on the alert.

"Why?" I ask, the word echoing loudly in the still room.

"Nothing to worry about," my mother says reassuringly. "I just want to find out why I'm feeling so tired lately. No doubt the doctor will give me a prescription for multivitamins or vitamin D."

"But you already take vitamins!" I splutter. My mother is meticulous when it comes to ingesting her daily nutrients.

She shrugs. "Maybe my body isn't absorbing the brand I'm using now," she says. "It could be I need a different type, or maybe I'm missing a specific vitamin that I need to take in extra doses."

I glide back and forth in the rocking chair, trying to imbibe some comfort from the smooth motion. Could a lack of vitamins really make someone feel so sleepy all the time?

My eyes narrow. Maybe there's something else my mother isn't telling me. Maybe she's suffering from other symptoms, too. She's the last person to run to the doctor simply because she's tired!

My mind is whirling with horrifying, frightening options, each one worse than the one before. I am about to confront my mother, beg her to tell me what's *really* going on, when —

Rrrriiinngg.

The noise is jarring in the quiet room, and we both jump.

I sigh. The moment has been lost. My mother will no doubt lapse into a long conversation with one of my sisters — I'm sure it's one of them calling, after all — and I will end up trudging upstairs to my room to hack my way through the mounds of homework that the teachers continue to dispense, even during production season.

"Hello?" my mother says. Her eyes widen, but she's smiling. "Sure, hold on a minute." She hands the phone to me. "Brachie, it's for you."

I stare at her for a moment, more than a little surprised. The phone call is for *me*? Then I remember that Ricki and Zehava asked us to practice our lines at home, specifically with the girls who appear most often with us on stage. I accept the phone, a shy smile on my face.

"Hello?" I say, expecting to hear Atara Gold's clear lilt.

"Hi, Brachie?" The voice is slightly raspy and hesitant.

I frown. Who could this be? "Yes?" I say expectantly, my mind running through the possibilities.

"It's Devora," she says nervously. I can't blame her for sounding so timid. It must have taken a lot of courage to call the principal's house and then have to speak to the principal herself.

"Oh, hi, Devora!" If I'm slightly disappointed, I don't let on.

"I was wondering...I mean...did you start the science homework yet?"

I shake my head, then realize Devora can't see me. "I didn't do any homework yet," I say.

My mother stands up with another yawn, a sign that she's ready for bed. It's time for me to get started on my homework — and for her to go to sleep. From my earliest memories, my mother has always been busy, busy, busy with a million and one tasks to tend to in the evening hours. I look at her now, my brow furrowed in consternation.

"I know you ate in school," my mother whispers to me. "But I left food for you in the oven in case you're still hungry."

"One minute, Devora, okay?" I cover the mouthpiece of the phone. "Thanks," I tell my mother. "Maybe I'll eat it later. If I decide not to, I'll put it in the fridge soon."

CURTAIN CALL • 111

As I head upstairs, my knapsack on my back and the phone in my hand, I wonder if I'll be able to ingest a single bite of food until I know just what the doctor has to say about my mother's condition.

Atara

"How'd it go?" my mother asks me as I step into the house at the end of a long day.

I shrug. "It was okay, I guess."

"Did you get to practice your part, or were you just listening to everyone else read hers?"

I have the grace to blush. Last year I had complained non-stop about all the time I was wasting, just sitting there watching everyone else perform. Of course, in order to have a play, everyone has to practice at some point. And there would be future rehearsals that would require only certain girls to attend, while the heads worked with them to hone their performance. But still…

"I read some of my lines," I say. "Nothing major, though. We're still breaking into it."

My mother nods. "I saved you some vegetable soup. Do you want?"

I brighten instantly. "Thanks. Of course I do!" My mother's vegetable soup is filling and delicious, and I am instantly hungry all over again.

My mother sits at the table with me, while Janet putters around washing dishes and making sure the kitchen is sparkling clean.

"Where are the girls?" I ask.

"They're upstairs, playing in their room," my mother says. "I told them you'd come in to say goodnight when you come home."

That's definitely one of the perks of having such a big house. My little sisters don't even know I'm downstairs, and I can have a few minutes of quiet before I go up to wish them goodnight and am cajoled into reading "just one more" book to them.

"I'm tired," my mother says, stifling a yawn. The diamonds on her fingers glint brightly in the white light of the modern light fixtures above our heads.

"Oh?" I say, savoring the steamy warmth of the soup.

"We worked hard today on the Chinese auction," my mother says, her eyes half-closing with satisfaction. "We got a lot done... but there's still a whole lot more to do!"

I nod. I'm in no mood to hear about the auction, about which vendors are donating which exclusive items, or which shade of burgundy was chosen to best display the one-of-a-kind wares. At some point, I know, I'll be enlisted to help brainstorm and come up with creative ideas guaranteed to blow the crowd away. I always relish the attention my mothers' friends lavish on me, and I enjoy being behind the scenes of one of the main community events each year.

But at the same time, I feel a constant prickle of resentment when it comes to the Chinese auction. It takes up so much of my mother's time, keeping her away from the family for hours on end each week. Already, I can tell, my mother's energies are focused on the auction, though the event itself is still months away. The thought is disquieting, to say the least.

A silence falls over the table, punctuated by an occasional

splash of water as Janet runs the *fleishig* faucet. I watch her aimlessly as I steadily empty out my bowl. My little sisters accept Janet as an addendum to the family; she's been a part of our life almost since they were born. Her slight but strong form moves energetically as she scrubs a dish, achieving the shimmery sparkle that my mother likes so much.

I remember watching my mother doing dishes herself when I was little. It looked like fun, and I used to ask if I could lather the dishes alongside her. "When you're bigger," my mother would tell me fondly.

Except now I'm bigger — much bigger — and I'm still not doing dishes. My friends envy what they call my "lazy life," but sometimes I wonder if my family wouldn't be more content in our simpler life, the way we lived it way back when. For all that Janet is supposed to make our lives easier, somehow my parents are that much busier these days...

I push back my bowl, which is now empty, and carelessly drop the spoon inside. It clatters loudly. I stand up and bring the bowl over to Janet to wash. She nods at me.

"Thanks," I tell her, feeling somewhat uncomfortable that she's doing something for me that I could have easily done myself.

My mother stands up as well, scrolling through the call log on her cell phone. Just then, the cordless phone rings on the gleaming countertop. My mother, who is closest to it, answers.

"Hello?" she says. "Sure, hold on a minute, please."

She hands me the phone, and I try to guess who it is. Although all our phones are graced with the convenience of caller ID, I enjoy guessing who might be on the other line.

I shmoozed with Yocheved and Malkie on my way out of school just before, so I doubt it's one of them calling now. And I caught a ride home with Chana Rochel's mother, so I don't think it's her on the phone so soon either.

Then I remember how the heads told us to practice our lines together with other cast members. It makes sense for Brachie Bodner and me to rehearse together, to fine-tune our parts as best as we can before we actually get to the next rehearsal, which is only two nights away.

I'm pleasantly surprised that Brachie is taking the initiative and reaching out to me. Maybe these rehearsals will go better than expected, after all.

"Hello?" I say expectantly.

"Hi, Atara." The voice is more high-pitched than Brachie's smooth tones, and I am momentarily confused. "It's Penina."

"Oh, hi." I try to imbue some warmth into my voice, hoping my lack of enthusiasm isn't too noticeable. "What's doing?"

"Nothing much," she says. "I was just wondering if you have a minute to help me with the Chumash homework."

I look at my mother, who already has her phone tucked between her ear and chin. I glance at Janet, who is now wiping down the sink. There isn't much else for me to do in this kitchen.

"Fine," I say, shrugging even though Penina can't see me. "Just give me a minute to get to my room, okay?"

I trudge up the stairs, passing my sisters' room where they are busy chatting and giggling together. I will wish them goodnight as soon as I get off the phone — which should be fairly quickly, I hope. Then I turn into my own bedroom, flick on the light, and get to work.

CHAPTER 14

Brachie

Today's the day.

Today my mother, *limudei kodesh* principal of Bais Breindel, will exit school, her oversized, black leather pocketbook swinging from her shoulder. She will climb into her trusty blue Camry and drive over to the doctor's office. She'll sit in the waiting room for who-knows-how-long, until the secretary ushers her into one of the examination rooms. And then, after some more interminable waiting, the doctor will finally come in...and he will try to get to the bottom of my mother's malaise.

This scenario is running through my head, each time with slightly different variations, making it awfully hard for me to sit through class after class. Even when recess time comes and the classroom becomes filled with the sounds of animated conversation, I remain immersed in my thoughts, present in body but not really in spirit.

I jump when I hear someone saying my name. I feel as if I am being tugged back from a different world, the world of the mind, where imagination runs rampant and anything can happen. With a sigh, I look up at the cause of my interruption — and am startled to see Atara Gold standing over me.

"Oh!" I say, taken aback. "Um..."

Atara steps in without preamble, before I can make any excuses for my discombobulated state of mind. "I was thinking," she says, "that we should practice our lines together tonight. We're having another rehearsal tomorrow, and I know Ricki and Zehava really want us to work together before that."

I don't know what to say. How can I spend my night on an activity as mundane as rehearsing lines for a play, when my mother's life might be hanging in the balance?

"Um..."

Atara is looking at me, and the ball is clearly in my court.

"I guess...I need to ask my mother."

"Okay," Atara says agreeably. "Why don't you go ask her?"

I just look at her, not sure what she wants from me.

"Isn't your mother usually in her office now?" Atara asks pointedly.

I flush. Good point. I look down at my watch. It's only ten thirty-five. My mother isn't leaving school for another hour. I'm sure my mother will tell me that of course, tonight is a horrible night to rehearse for the play, that she needs me home with her. And if the principal says no, Atara Gold surely can't argue with that.

I stand up and make my way out of the classroom. Suddenly, I remember something. Feeling foolish, I catch Atara's eye. She is still standing in the same spot, watching me, and I am discomfited.

I retrace my steps hesitantly, my cheeks burning. "Um…" I say, trying to call upon my usual poise. "You wanted to practice at your house, right?"

Atara nods. "Yeah, I thought you could come over straight after school. I'll double-check with my mother, but it shouldn't be a problem."

I nod in turn. Of course. I couldn't expect her to come to the principal's house — and I don't even want her to. Sighing, feeling like I'm being cornered into this, I turn to leave the classroom and head toward my mother's office.

Signs of production are all over the place. Girls are clustered in the hallway, some humming songs they have recently learned. Others are showing off some new dance steps.

As I exit the stairwell, I catch sight of the production bulletin board. It's strange how, just two days ago, all I could care about was which part I was getting. Now, faced with far more pressing and serious concerns, I don't even bother to give the bulletin board more than a cursory glance.

"Hi," I say to Mrs. Blothstein, the secretary. "Is my mother in her office?"

Mrs. Blothstein's fingers fly over the keyboard, and I marvel at how she can look up at me while still typing.

"She is," the secretary confirms. "But she's meeting with someone now."

"Is it a long meeting?" I want to know.

Mrs. Blothstein shrugs and smiles. "You know how it goes," she murmurs vaguely before turning back to her computer.

I stand outside my mother's door, hoping it isn't a fellow student inside. It would be horrid if my mother were chastising some poor girl, and this girl came out to see The Principal's Daughter standing right there, seemingly the model of everything a perfect student should be. The girl would no doubt resent me, especially if she were in my grade; maybe she'd even make some snide remark about goody-goodies or something like that.

I squirm, knowing that I'm getting carried away with my thoughts once again.

A moment later, I can hear the door opening and my mother's soothing yet authoritative voice. A few moments later, Morah Bulman steps out. She smiles when she sees me.

I smile back, while cringing inwardly. I can't help but wonder what she was discussing with my mother.

"Oh, Brachie!" my mother says, surprised. I don't come to visit her often in school, and for a second I feel guilty about that.

"Uh, can I come in, Ima?" My eyes are darting all around, making sure no one is watching. I prefer to downplay our relationship as much as possible when in public.

"Sure." My mother closes the door behind us and waits for me to talk.

"I...I wanted to know..." I pause and look around the small but neat office, not sure how to phrase my request. After all, *I'm* not the one who wanted to ask it. It's Atara who put me up to this. Confused, I begin again. "Um...Atara Gold asked me if we could practice our lines together tonight. At her house."

My mother smiles, and I can tell she's trying to mask her delight. "Sure, that sounds like a great idea."

"Um...are you sure?" I venture. "I mean, you're going to the doctor and all."

My mother looks confused. "What does that have to do with anything?"

I flush, feeling once again like a fool. "Well...won't you want to have me home tonight? Like, maybe he'll tell you something..." I am stammering uncontrollably, mentally kicking myself for not being upfront with my mother.

She's your mother! a little voice admonishes me. *You can talk to her normally.*

I'm gratified when my mother's eyes widen in understanding. "Oh, Brachie, I told you already — there's really nothing to worry about," she says reassuringly. "I'm just going for a checkup, really, and I assume he'll send me for some blood work. But that could take a couple of days."

"Oh." I feel deflated. All this tension I've been feeling — and it's going to stretch on for a few more days?! How horrible.

"I'm sure everything's fine," my mother tells me for the umpteenth time. "Go to Atara's house, and enjoy yourself. Okay?"

"Okay," I agree miserably. Despite my mother's reassurances, I'm still worried.

My mother looks down at her watch. "Recess is almost over," she says. "You'd better hurry back to class, or you might need a late note from the principal." Her eyes are twinkling, but, unsurprisingly, I don't think it's so funny.

It's only when I'm trudging back up the stairs that I realize my mission has gone unaccomplished. I have absolutely no desire to spend the night with Atara Gold — and I'm desperate for a way to get out of it.

Atara

I'M A MATH TYPE OF PERSON. There's something about the neat, logical order of numbers that appeals to me. I like how the digits line up in rows, how the answer is always derived from a straightforward mathematical computation. Especially today, when the whiteboard is covered with all kinds of geometric shapes and perfect-looking angles, I'd expect myself to be absolutely engrossed in the lesson.

But I'm not, and there's a very good reason for it: Brachie Bodner.

I'm frowning as I copy Miss Gluck's latest example into my notebook. Why, I wonder for what seems like the millionth time, is Brachie so reluctant to come to my house?

My mind flits back to recess earlier that day, when I approached Brachie's desk. She seemed so hesitant, so reluctant, to have anything to do with me.

Does she look down upon me, because my family is so different from hers? Maybe she views me as too ostentatious for her tastes, too busy with trinkets and baubles?

The thought saddens me. I've always respected Brachie Bodner — looked up to her, even. The notion that she looks upon me as less than herself is disheartening, to say the least.

I shift in my seat, and it creaks. I'm regretting that I ever invited Brachie to my house tonight. But how will we give the play our best if we can't get together and practice our lines?

I toy with the idea of asking Brachie if she'd like *me* to go to *her* house, then nix it a moment later. For all that I'm aching with curiosity to get a firsthand view of how Mrs. Bodner lives,

CURTAIN CALL • 121

there's no way I'd have the guts to step over her threshold and meet my principal in the intimate setting of her home.

I have no choice but to hope that tonight proceeds uneventfully. And the truth is, really, what could go wrong?

I fiddle with my pencil, trying to think if there's any other reason why Brachie might bear a grudge against me. If on Sunday I thought she looked at me as competition — well, our roles have already been assigned. She can't blame me for usurping a position in the play from her; our roles are pretty much the same size.

Besides, I always thought Brachie was beyond these things. Just look at who her mother is — the paradigm of perfection, practically! Of course, I've sat through enough *hashkafah* lessons to know that only Hashem is perfect. But still, Mrs. Bodner is a pretty special lady — warm and approachable, yet always dignified and commanding respect.

I find it hard to believe that Brachie could be so different from her mother, *middos*-wise. We've been classmates since my family moved to this city, back when I was a pigtailed second grader, and my earliest memories of Brachie are all overwhelmingly positive. So what, then, could be bothering Brachie?

Miss Gluck is announcing tonight's homework assignment, which means that class is dwindling to a close. The thought makes me wish the bell won't ring for another...well, for forever, really. Because when it does, I've got to take Brachie Bodner home with me.

Brachie

THE FIRST THING I NOTICE when I step through the ornate front door of Atara Gold's house is the mirrors. Two entire walls of the majestic entranceway are covered with mirrors. I once read that mirrors are an interior decorator's secret to creating a big space from a small one, and I can't help but wonder why this foyer would need to seem any more impressive than it already is.

I look around in wonder. Atara, at my side, is unusually quiet, but I'm too busy being awestruck to wonder about that for more than a few passing seconds

"Can I take your coat?" Atara asks me.

I wordlessly give her my gray coat, handed down from Shifra. I liked it enough when Shifra first offered it to me, but right now, in these elegant surroundings, I feel positively dowdy in it.

Atara opens a door camouflaged by mirrors. I peek in behind her and gasp. There's an enormous closet hiding there — an entire room, really, and I am mesmerized. I think fleetingly of my family's tiny, front-hall closet. It suits us just fine now, but I well remember how jam-packed it was when all my siblings still lived at home.

"Well?" Atara says when she emerges from the closet-room. "Shall we start?"

I nod, and Atara leads me toward a wide, majestic staircase. Just then, a well-dressed woman wearing a blonde, shoulder-length *sheitel* walks toward us, her heels clacking loudly on the marble floor.

"Tari! Hello!" she says.

Atara turns around and smiles — rather stiffly, I think.

"Hi, Mommy," she says. "This is Brachie Bodner. We're practicing for the play together."

"Hi, Brachie!" Mrs. Gold says, flashing a wide, warm smile in my direction. "How nice to meet you."

Atara is shifting from foot to foot, casting longing glances at the staircase. I wonder what's bothering her, why she's so anxious to get away from her mother. Mrs. Gold seems so sweet and sincere.

"Do you have a minute, Atara?" Mrs. Gold asks. "Some of my friends are over, and I'd like you to say hello to them."

I peek at Atara. The expression on her face seems frozen, but then she thaws and smiles. "Sure, Mommy." She turns to me. "Sorry," she whispers apologetically.

I'm not sure if I should follow her or not, but surely she doesn't mean to leave me standing alone at the foot of the grand staircase. Atara turns around just then to make sure I'm behind her. Reassured, I walk slowly, taking in my surroundings with wide eyes.

We pass a living room that looks like it was copied and pasted straight out of a magazine ad, and I doubt anyone has ever sat on the pristine, antique-style sofas. The next set of double doors reveals a gleaming dining room set and breakfront filled with more valuables than the most prominent of silver stores. Mrs. Gold is heading down another hallway, passing a dark-skinned woman carrying a mop. I can't help but wonder if this is the cleaning lady or a live-in.

Finally, after passing several more doors, which I would have loved to peek behind, Mrs. Gold leads us into what must be a den. It's beautifully decorated, with gorgeous paintings and leather couches that perfectly match the large rug on the floor and the tasseled curtains hanging from the window. But that's not what I notice first.

My eyes are glued to the three elegant women seated on the couches. Gucci handbags are strewn casually around the floor, and a spiral notebook sits prominently on the glass coffee table.

"Hi, Atara!" one of the women says, with a toss of her perfectly-coiffed black *sheitel*.

"Hi," Atara replies. I can't help noticing how her smile doesn't reach her eyes.

"Care to join our planning meeting?" a woman with a thick, diamond-studded choker asks, winking.

"I'd love to," Atara says politely, "but I'm supposed to be rehearsing right now." She gestures to me, and I smile uncomfortably.

"What's your name?" the third woman asks me. She has a wavy, auburn *sheitel* and sparkling, emerald eyes.

I am momentarily flustered but quickly call upon my acting abilities to help me out here. "Brachie Bodner," I reply.

"Bodner," the woman murmurs. "As in…" She pauses, thinking for a moment.

I shift uncomfortably from foot to foot, knowing what is coming.

"…Mrs. Bodner, principal of Bais Breindel?" she finishes.

I nod, well aware of the fact that my cheeks are flaming.

"How nice," the woman says, looking approvingly at me. "You must know my daughter, then — Tziri Cohen, in the ninth grade?"

"Yes," I say, then clear my throat uncomfortably. I feel myself blush even more, if that is at all possible.

"Well," Atara cuts in, "we're going to go practice our lines now."

"Oh, production season!" the woman with the black *sheitel* says excitedly.

"The things you miss out on when you have only boys," Mrs. Cohen jokes to her. I can hear the other women laughing good-naturedly as we leave the room.

Atara walks quickly, agitatedly, and I wonder what's bothering her. Her mother's friends are so nice; what could she have against them?

"They're planning a Chinese auction for a *chessed* organization," Atara tells me tersely, almost tripping over her words in the rush to get them out.

I'm impressed. It's so nice that these ladies — all of them obviously blessed with wealth — are using their time and resources to help raise much-needed money for *tzedakah*.

Atara leads me down a thickly-carpeted hallway, then into her room. I stare, stunned, at the spectacle in front of me. This room could also have been transplanted straight out of a magazine ad. It's absolutely beautiful, breathtaking, and I can only imagine how many delightful hours Atara must while away in this cocoon of luxury.

As my shoes sink deeper into the soft lavender carpet, I am annoyed, to put it mildly, at what I am feeling. Could it be… that I, who was taught from a tender age that extras in life are not what bring happiness…am I *jealous* of Atara Gold?

Atara

WHY, OH, WHY, did Mommy have to pick tonight, of all nights, to host her clique of friends? I can't remember ever being so embarrassed. These women are so different from Mrs. Bodner and the women she surely associates with, that the contrast is almost laughable. What must Brachie *think*?

I wonder if Brachie is pondering why these women are at my house now, when their children must be home from school. I'm sure Brachie's own mother is in her house every day when she comes home from school — that's just the type of person she is. Maybe I should explain to her that Mrs. Levy's boys are all in yeshivah until later; that Mrs. Cohen brought her younger children along with her and they are playing with my sisters in the basement right now; and that Mrs. Kenigsberg's kids are busy after school with a host of different lessons — art, piano, and ice skating?

I am about to clarify to Brachie just how these ladies of leisure can afford to spend this normally hectic hour sitting in my den, when I pause. I don't want Brachie to think that I feel the need to excuse myself — even if I do.

Instead, I turn to her with a forced smile. "Let's get started," I say.

I notice that Brachie is taking in the ceiling-to-floor drapes, the lilac furniture, the throw pillows scattered at the head of my bed, the matching beanbags perched at perfect angles on the floor. I am tense, waiting for a hint of disapproval, for some sign of how my estimation is sliding down a slippery slope in Brachie's eyes.

But she says nothing — and really, I'm not shocked. She's an actress, after all, just like me. My eyes suddenly glint, and I throw my shoulders back. I'm an actress, too, and there's no reason Brachie should detect any sign of unease on my part. Two can play this game, can they not?

"Okay," I say, with a confidence that I don't feel at the moment. "Maria, take out your script and tell me what exactly Don Mendeles is doing wrong!"

Brachie looks at me, surprised, but then giggles. "Okay," she says agreeably, bending down to her knapsack.

The atmosphere in the room has just defrosted by several degrees, and I heave a sigh of relief. I exhale slowly, then smile to myself and take out my own script. It's time to rehearse.

CHAPTER 15

Brachie

THE FIRST THING I NOTICE when Mrs. Kenigsberg, one of Mrs. Gold's fancy friends who so graciously offered me a ride home, pulls up in front of my house, is the presence of my father's battered Taurus in the driveway. I am instantly alarmed. Why is he home so early? His job as a *mashgiach* in a yeshivah usually has him putting in late hours. What could possibly be pulling him away from "his" boys?

Maybe something happened to my mother? Maybe…maybe the doctor arrived at a diagnosis already, despite my mother's assurances that it would certainly take at least a few days to receive any results?

"Th-thank you," I manage to say to Mrs. Kenigsberg. My fingers are shaking so much that I can barely manage to pull open the door of her minivan.

I fairly run up the walkway and pound on the door. My father pulls it open a moment later.

"Hi, Brachie," he says. "Why are you knocking so loudly? Where's your key?"

"Where's Ima?" I blurt out, looking around in alarm.

"Brachie?" My father peers worriedly at me. "Is everything okay?"

"I don't know!" I cry. My heart is beating wildly, and my eyes are darting in all directions, seeking out my mother. "Where's Ima?"

"What's going on?" my mother asks, coming down the stairs. She looks from me to my father, confused. "Why is there so much noise?"

I nearly sag against the wall in relief, dumping my knapsack to the ground in the process. "Y-you're okay!" I manage to say, through the pounding in my head.

"*Baruch Hashem*," my mother says, sounding bemused. The next moment I hear a sharp intake of breath as she realizes what's going on. "Brachie," my mother says, her eyes narrowed, "I told you already that everything is fine."

"What did the doctor say?" I ask anxiously.

"Exactly what I thought he would — that I need to take my vitamins and I should do some blood work to rule out anything else."

"Anything else?" I echo, my eyes wide.

My mother shakes her head as if I'm a hopeless case and looks at my father.

"Brachie," my father puts in, "Ima's symptoms are not worrisome at all. There's really no reason to be so alarmed. Maybe she really isn't getting enough sleep, or maybe she has some type of virus that's making her so sleepy. Whatever it is, we're going to get to the bottom of it."

I glance from my father to my mother, not at all convinced. "So why are you home now?" I ask my father, almost accusingly.

He smiles. "The Katzes from down the block are making a wedding tonight, remember?"

I look at my mother, who, I suddenly realize, is wearing her Shabbos *sheitel* and elegant black suit. I shake my head, feeling slightly foolish. No, I hadn't remembered about that wedding.

"Do you have the strength to go to a wedding?" I ask my mother, feeling silly. Right now, I sound like *I'm* the fretful mother.

She smiles calmly at me. "*Baruch Hashem.*"

I shrug. It's not like she'd tell me if she wasn't feeling up to it, and it's also not like her to stay home and miss her friend's daughter's wedding.

"We won't be out so late," my mother tells me. She stifles a yawn.

I can only stare at her, trying to quash down the feeling of alarm that is, once again, spreading through my limbs, despite my parents' reassurances. Why is my mother yawning? It's only seven thirty, hardly late at all.

I watch as my parents put on their coats. Is it my imagination, or does my mother seem pale? Maybe it's just the pallor of her face showing up against the flush of her makeup? Or perhaps we just need new lighting in the hall?

"Whatever," I mumble, not realizing I've said the word aloud.

"Did you say something?" my mother asks, her eyebrows raised.

"No," I say, sighing.

"By the way, Brachie," my mother says, pulling on her gloves. "I forgot to ask you — how'd it go by Atara's house?"

"It was fine," I say.

I'm amazed to find that I actually mean it. Our mini rehearsal went well, and I'm starting to think that Ricki and Zehava were on to something, after all. Maybe Atara Gold and I *do* have some sort of chemistry.

"Good," my mother says, satisfied. "I'm glad. Atara is a very sweet girl."

I agree with my mother's assessment — but I'm *not* at all pleased to hear her voice it. I wish that my mother didn't know all the girls in my class; didn't know all the ins and outs of our production; didn't know everything and anything about what goes on in the halls of Bais Breindel.

I wish my mother wasn't the principal.

Feeling slightly disloyal, I walk up to my mother and give her a kiss. She looks caught off-guard by this unexpected show of affection, but reciprocates in turn.

Then I wish goodnight to both my parents and shut the door behind them.

Atara

"Daddy's home! Daddy's home!"

The cries of delight catch me by surprise as I try to make sense of the scientific terms splashed all over my textbook. Grateful for an excuse to take a break — and happy to see my father home so early, for once — I fairly skip out of my room and down the wide, yawning staircase.

My sisters are dancing around my father, little, lively bursts of sunlight in this huge, sprawling house. My father hugs them.

"Hi, Daddy," I say, smiling from the sidelines.

My father smiles back and waves to me. Then he turns to someone standing off to the side. "Can I take your coat?" he offers.

I am startled as I take in a very tall, thin man. Although he is well-dressed, in a tailored suit and expensive-looking tie, his willowy build reminds me of a scarecrow. I eye the man, wondering why I haven't noticed him until now.

"Who are you?" Miri asks the man, with the sweet innocence unique to little children.

"I'm your dad's friend," the tall man replies, his eyes crinkling at the corners like he's telling a good joke.

I glance at my mother. Something about this man is off-putting...but what is it, exactly? His height? The slight hint of a drawl beneath his New York accent?

My mother is poised, as usual, with a polite expression on her face. I can't tell what she's thinking, or if she *is* thinking anything particularly pressing. My father is not usually prone to bringing home friends at this time of night, it's true, but so what? Haven't stranger things happened?

Still, I am quiet as I watch my father interact with this unexpected guest. Although he is his usual affable self, he seems somehow a bit tense at the same time. I wonder if it's the way his shoulders are set, or the smile that refuses to leave his face for even a moment.

Or maybe I'm just imagining the whole thing.

"This is Mr. Steinhaurt," my father tells us.

Mr. Steinhaurt flashes a smile in our direction, and there is a slightly awkward silence after that.

"Can we eat supper all over again, now that Daddy is home?" Esti asks eagerly.

My mother shakes her head. "You girls have to go to sleep now."

"Please?" Elisheva begs.

My mother glances at my father, then bites her lip. "Daddy and Mr. Steinhaurt are going to eat together," she says.

I wonder why there's an emphasis on the "together" — and why my mother seems so uncomfortable.

"Come, kids," I say, taking Miri and Esti by the hand. I want to beat a retreat myself, and taking my little sisters with me is the perfect excuse. "Who wants me to read her a book?"

"Me!" three high-pitched voices chorus.

My mother sends me a grateful look. But, to my surprise, instead of heading to the kitchen to sit with my father when he eats, like she usually does, she comes upstairs and follows me into my sisters' room.

I pull Miri onto my lap while Elisheva chooses a book from the bookcase. I start to read, casting surreptitious glances at my mother while she glides back and forth, back and forth, on the rocking chair in the corner of the room. It creaks loudly as she continues to sway, faster and faster.

My mother is not looking in our direction. Instead, her eyes are half-closed, and she looks worried.

Very worried.

CHAPTER 16

Brachie

I'VE ALWAYS LIKED ROSH CHODESH — and it's not just because we get to miss class on account of the school assembly we always have then. There's something alluring about starting a new month, a hint of new opportunities and choices that are there for the taking. All in all, I'm feeling pretty upbeat as I sit back in my seat in the enormous auditorium, waiting for the assembly to begin.

All around me, girls are chatting, laughing, exchanging animated hellos with other girls they haven't seen in forty-five minutes, as if forty-five days have passed instead. I relax, allowing my thoughts to fast-forward to the rehearsal that will be held tonight.

I'm excited about it. I think Zehava and Ricki will be duly impressed with the progress Atara and I made last night at her house. And I'm starting to realize that a good actress can take any part assigned to her, however minor it may be, and hone it to perfection, until she shines and sparkles in the spotlight.

I am smiling to myself just as my mother steps up to the microphone.

Instantly, a hush settles over the auditorium. My mother scans the room, making eye contact with the girls spread out in neat rows. That's her way of ensuring she has everyone's attention.

Her eye catches mine, and I squirm, hoping no one noticed that slight interaction. The second passes, and my mother's gaze continues to flit over the room. Finally, she's ready.

"A *gut chodesh*, girls," she begins, smiling. I am tense, as I always am when my mother addresses the school. I've sat through countless assemblies and speeches of hers, but still, every time my mother speaks in front of the school, I wait impatiently for the ordeal to be over.

"Chodesh Shevat is a time of renewal," my mother says. She pauses, collecting her thoughts. "It's a time of *his'chadshus*. On Tu B'Shvat —"

My mother looks down and puts a hand to her head. I sit forward tensely, wondering what's going on, why her voice lacks its usual verve and vivacity.

I watch my mother give her head a little shake, then briefly close her eyes, as if trying to resume her thoughts. This is all so out of character for her that I am frozen, afraid, almost frantic. Why, I want to know, is my mother behaving so oddly?!

"Girls," my mother says, beginning again.

The room is still. We are all watching, waiting.

And then, to my horror, my mother, the esteemed principal of Bais Breindel, slowly slumps to the ground.

Atara

Pandemonium.

That's the only word that can describe what happens when Mrs. Bodner faints during the Rosh Chodesh assembly. Girls scream, others cry, and still others just sit there, looking dazed.

Morah Bulman is the first teacher to respond. "Call Hatzolah!" she shouts as she runs to Mrs. Bodner's limp form.

About twenty girls race to the office. Within minutes, we can hear the wail of sirens making their way to our school. The other teachers, trying to collect their wits, usher their students out of the auditorium.

Through all this mayhem, I try to find Brachie. Where could she be? How is she coping?

I am following my friends out of the auditorium when I turn around one last time, and I see her. Brachie is on the ground beside her mother, her face ashen and her eyes terrified.

Two men wielding walkie-talkies dash into the room. A teacher points them in Mrs. Bodner's direction, while another teacher makes sure there are no students left in the auditorium.

I walk dazedly to my classroom with my friends. The mood in the hallway is subdued and somber. No one is really talking. Girls look frightened and only whisper when they need to say something.

I follow Yocheved into our classroom, to find Devora already seated at her desk, saying Tehillim. Following her lead, the rest of us sit down quietly and pull out our *sifrei Tehillim*.

We don't even know Mrs. Bodner's full name, but we beseech Hashem to send our principal a *refuah sheleimah*. As I whisper the words, composed so long ago when Dovid Hamelech experienced incomprehensible *yissurim*, an image of Brachie, crouching forlornly beside her mother, springs to my mind.

Please, Hashem, I add, *give Brachie the strength to get through this.*

Brachie

THE SITUATION IS SURREAL. My house is so packed with people, you'd think we were hosting a party. All I want is for everyone to go home, so I can at least pretend that everything is fine and normal and nothing out of the ordinary happened that day. Instead, my sisters are going full steam ahead.

"Poor Brachie," Chevy says. "It must be so embarrassing for her."

"You know, I happen to be sitting right here," I say tersely. Why is she talking about me like I'm out of the room, instead of two feet away from her?

Ettie casts me a look smothered with sympathy, and it takes every ounce of my willpower to not bolt right out of the room.

Dassi sits back on the couch. "At least everything ended okay, *baruch Hashem*. Just forget about the embarrassing part, Brachie. In a few days, no one in school will remember what happened."

I grit my teeth. Who are my sisters to tell me how I should feel? Were they in school when my mother lost consciousness in front of an entire room filled with people? Are they the ones who will have to walk through the halls of Bais Breindel as The Daughter of the Principal Who Fainted?

I am thankful that my mother is okay — so, so thankful. But after processing the intense gratitude I feel, I experience a rush of emotion so strong, I have no idea how I will ever go back to school: humiliation.

My father enters the room just then, and my sisters pounce on him.

"How's Ima?" Shifra asks.

"She's sleeping," my father replies, looking like he could use a nap himself.

We all could use some rest, actually. I've waded in a frenzied daze through the hectic hours that passed since my mother's trip to the emergency room, and I know that I'm feeling rather like a limp ragdoll.

"So what happened, exactly?" Ettie asks.

My father sighs as he settles himself into an armchair. "Well, as we were told in the emergency room, it seems that Ima has mono," my father says. "It's not so common in adults, which is why no one thought to check for it in the first place. But that's why she's been so tired these past few weeks."

"But why'd Ima faint?" Shifra wants to know. "I never heard of anyone fainting from mono."

"Ima was feeling light-headed, because she didn't really eat this morning," my father tells us. "She didn't have much of an appetite, and she didn't get that much sleep last night, either;

we came home pretty late from the Katz *chasunah*."

I smile wryly to myself, remembering how I'd waited tensely for my parents to come home the night before. I don't usually mind being alone in the house, but I was feeling anxious about my mother, and the hours had stretched painfully before me. But never, in my worst-case imaginings, could I have envisioned what would happen this morning...

Mono. I exhale loudly as I lean back into a cushion. Such a simple diagnosis, but such a complicated day!

"So what now?" Chevy asks.

"Well, Ima will have to take it easy for a few weeks," my father says. He folds his arms and fixes his gaze on the wall. "She'll need to rest and stay in bed as much as she can."

"We'll all help out," Dassi assures him.

"Yes," Chevy says. "We'll take turns sending over supper. And Brachie will take care of the laundry and keeping the house clean."

I glower at my busybody sister. Of course I plan on helping out — but her condescending assumption that she can tell me what to do is too much.

Right now, this is all too much for me to process. And the crushing burden I carry, wondering what everyone in school is *thinking*, is suddenly overwhelming.

"Excuse me," I say. I stand up stiffly, trying to keep my dignity intact but knowing that I am failing. Then I flounce out of the room and up the stairs.

The door to my mother's room is open, and I can make out her sleeping form. I tread softly into my own room, lock the door behind me...and start to cry.

Atara

"Okay, I need Don and Dona Mendeles now," Ricki says. She looks at me. "Juanita, you're going to be pretending to clean while trying to hear the conversation going on in the sitting room. All right?"

I nod, although my heart isn't in it. It's strange and kind of pointless to be rehearsing without Brachie when we'd both gotten this part down pat the night before. We'd even come up with some bumbling moves sure to get a laugh out of the audience, and we were waiting for tonight to run them by Ricki and Zehava.

Well, that will have to wait a bit longer. I have more pressing concerns on my mind at the moment: how is Mrs. Bodner?

The teachers had assured us that our principal regained consciousness pretty quickly and is fine now. Still, there is no way for us to know if they were just glossing over things — and if what happened this morning is an indication of something really terrible.

I sigh as I peruse my script. I think of Brachie, and how I wish I could call her. Not because I want the inside scoop — she's far too private to ever give it to me, anyway — but just to let her know that I'm thinking of her.

I really am. We're not friends, Brachie and I, but we *have* been classmates for years, and we *will* be working closely together over the next month and a half. I wish there were some way I could impart my concern for her mother, my hope that everything is okay. But how to do it?

There's no way I could conjure up the courage to call the

Bodner household. For all I know, Mrs. Bodner is safely home and answering phone calls already. But what if I write Brachie a card?

Nah, I decide, that would be too tacky. Brachie would probably be confused as to why I was sending it, not touched.

I'm sure Brachie's friends will help her pull through this, I tell myself. *She doesn't need me at all.* But as I listen with half an ear to Zehava issuing some instructions on how we need to stand so we face the audience, I realize something:

I have no idea who Brachie Bodner calls her close friends.

CHAPTER 17

Brachie

I TIPTOE DOWN THE HALL, careful not to make a sound. My mother needs to rest, rest, and rest some more, and I am committed to helping her do just that.

"Brachie?" my mother calls to me.

Oops. Maybe I wasn't as quiet as I thought. "Yes?" I say, backtracking my steps.

"It's nine thirty already. What are you doing home?"

I am fumbling for something to say when my mother appears at the doorway of her room, wrapped in a robe. I stare at her, surprised.

My mother smiles, her face rather pale. "It's okay," she tells me. "I'm allowed to get out of bed."

"When are you going back to work?" I ask her.

"The doctor thinks I should be okay in a few weeks," she says. "After all, I've already been sick for a while without knowing it."

I look hesitantly at my mother. How am I going to broach the topic that is burning on my tongue?

"Brachie, you didn't tell me why you're still home," my mother reminds me. "Are you feeling okay?"

I turn away as hot tears spring to my eyes. All I can do is nod.

"So what's bothering you, then?" my mother wants to know.

"H-how...how can I ever go back to school?" The words tumble out of my mouth in a bitter heap. "And how can *you* ever go back to school? Who knows what people are saying about us?"

My mother is silent as she looks at me. I avoid her gaze and run my slippered foot over the slightly threadbare carpet.

"Brachie," she says finally, "your feelings are normal. It's okay to be embarrassed and afraid of what other people are thinking. But I just want you to remember that things happen — things that are out of our control — and that too is part of Hashem's plan. The only thing that *is* in our control is how we deal with it."

The tears splash down my cheeks as I stand there miserably. I know my mother is right — and I know that *she* has much more reason to be embarrassed than me. But knowing her, she'll bounce right back into her job when the time is right, refusing to be pulled down by any feelings of humiliation she might have. Whereas for me...

"It's too hard for me!" I wail. "I know that everyone's going to be whispering behind my back, talking about me and you and about what happened. And who knows what kind of rumors are flying around already?"

I can feel my mother's arm around my shoulder, and I sob like a helpless baby. I haven't cried on my mother like this since...well, since I can't remember. And even though I'm hurting, something feels so *right*, so good.

My mother sighs. "Once I'm back in school, I think everyone will realize that I'm feeling just fine, *baruch Hashem*. People do pass out, you know. These things happen."

"Not during assemblies!" I cry. "And not to the principals who are supposed to be leading them."

My mother sighs again. "That, too, is part of His plan," she murmurs, more to herself than to me.

"It's hard enough that everyone looks at me like I'm different," I grouse. "Mrs. Bodner's daughter — be careful around her! She might go reporting back to the principal!"

The minute the words are out of my mouth, I wish I could stuff them right back in. How can I burden my mother like this when she's not feeling well? If yesterday was difficult for me, it was a million times more excruciating for her. And *she's* the one who has to spend weeks languishing in bed — not me.

I am mentally kicking myself as my mother's grip around me tightens. "You know, Brachie," she says slowly. "I—"

Just then the front door opens and closes, and a few moments later, my father is heading up the stairs.

"Brachie?" he says, confused. "Why are you home now?"

I shrug and swipe at my moist cheeks.

My father turns to my mother. "Is everything okay?" he asks.

"*Baruch Hashem*," my mother says calmly. "Brachie wants to

stay home today, and that's okay with me."

I am grateful when my father doesn't press further. I wriggle out of my mother's grasp and head downstairs to eat some breakfast.

I'm sure my parents are discussing me right now in the privacy of their room, but I'm too drained — and upset — to care. No amount of discussion could ever come up with a resolution for this issue. There is absolutely no solution to my problem — at least, nothing that I could think of. There seems to be no way out.

One day, I know, I'll have to go back to school, face the stares and the sympathetic glances, deal with the curiosity and the fallout from yesterday morning. But right now, I just can't see it happening.

Atara

THE SKY IS OVERCAST as I head home from school, Malkie at my side. We are supposed to be studying for tomorrow's Chumash test, but right now I wish we had scheduled our study session at Malkie's house instead of mine.

True, Malkie shares a room with a sister and her house is noisier than mine, but I'm not sure my house is where I want to be right now. I can't help remembering my mother's gloomy expression as I left for school this morning, and I just don't know what to expect when I come back home.

I try to pay attention to Malkie as we walk up my block.

"I wonder what's going on with Mrs. Bodner," she is saying, sticking her hands deep into her pockets. "Do you think it's true that she's really okay?"

I shrug. "I hope so. I'm sure she is, if the teachers said so."

"Still, why did she pass out?" Malkie presses.

"People pass out sometimes, don't they?" I am growing irritated, though I don't know why. Maybe it's the tension I'm feeling in my own house that doesn't allow me to concentrate on other people's troubles?

"Hey, maybe you can find out from Brachie," Malkie says excitedly. "Aren't you busy rehearsing with her?"

"We haven't really rehearsed too much yet," I tell Malkie. "Besides, I'm not really friends with her. I can't just ask her about what happened. It's not nice."

"I know you, Atara," Malkie says teasingly. "I'm sure you'll be able to ask her in a way that will catch her off-guard."

I blanch as Malkie's words hit me full-force in the face. Is that how my friends think of me? Do they think I'm conniving and sneaky, or does Malkie mean something else?

There's only one way to find out. "What do you mean?" I ask guardedly.

Malkie's laugh rings in the frigid, late afternoon air. "Oh, you know," she says blithely. "Everyone knows you're so charming...you know how to get whatever you want."

I'm frowning as I press the intercom outside the front door. That's not exactly how I want others to see me — or how I want to see myself.

"Hi," I call as we enter the front hall.

I can hear the drone of a vacuum upstairs, and Elisheva saying something loudly somewhere toward the back of the house. Malkie and I hang up our coats and then head to the kitchen for a snack.

Sure enough, my sisters are seated around the table, eating meatballs and spaghetti. My mother is perched beside them, looking somewhat distracted.

"Oh, hi, Atara!" she says, jumping up. "I didn't hear you come in. Hi, Malkie, how are you?"

"Great, *baruch Hashem*," Malkie replies, smiling.

"Do you girls want something to eat?" my mother asks.

"Just a snack," I say. "We'll eat supper later."

"Um…okay," my mother says, a pucker appearing between her eyes. "Just not too late, okay? Daddy's bringing home a friend for supper."

"Again?" I say. I want to ask other questions, too, but the pinched expression on my mother's face holds me back. I want to know why no one can join my father when he hosts his friend, unlike when we have other guests and the whole family eats together. I want to know if he's hosting the same friend as yesterday, or if there'll be a new guest today. Most of all, I want to know why my mother looks so strained.

My mother doesn't answer me as she putters around the kitchen. "Why don't you girls have something light now — there's a tray of cut-up fruit in the fridge."

"Sounds yum," Malkie says agreeably.

We sit down at the table, munching on honeydew and cantaloupe. The sweet fruit is refreshing after a long day at school, but I hardly notice what I'm eating. All I want is to know what, exactly, is going on inside our big, beautiful home.

Brachie

LONELINESS. It's pecking at me, coating me, making me wish desperately for human contact.

The house has been silent all day, save for the occasional phone calls from my sisters, wanting to know how my mother is feeling. My brothers called during their lunch break at yeshivah to inquire after her welfare, as well. And, of course, my father called repeatedly to check up on us both.

Throughout it all, my mother mostly slept. During the periods when she was up, I visited her in her room, but both of us avoided the elephant in the corner — how I am going to cope with going back to school, and when exactly I'm going to do so.

I stare out the window, noting how the day is receding into dusky evening, with only faint purple patches of sky letting the world know that it was ever lit up to begin with. The day has marched on without me, and I feel a twinge of sadness. Girls went to school, sat through class, chatted through recess, no doubt speculated about Mrs. Bodner's well-being, and then returned home once again to tackle their homework and mesh back into their families.

But not me. I haven't been part of any of this today. I am feeling sorry for myself. The house is still and silent. No friends are calling me, nor do I expect them to.

If only someone would express an interest in my life, in how I'm coping...but who would? Who would willingly call Mrs. Bodner's house, especially the day after she lost consciousness in front of the whole school? I can't blame anyone for shying away from such a prospect. But, in my heart of hearts, I also know that there is no one to call me anyway.

I huddle on the sofa, wrapped in solitude, when the doorbell shrills. Excitedly, I jump up and run to the door. "Who's there?" I call. I am so eager to see another face that I fling the door open, without waiting for a response.

My heart drops. Standing there, looking bemused, is Chevy.

Neither of us says anything for a long moment. Then Chevy finally asks, "Do you mind helping me? These bags are heavy."

I notice for the first time that she's holding two big shopping bags. I take one of them from her without saying a word.

"I made chicken soup for supper," Chevy says. "I figured Ima needs the nutrients."

"That's nice of you," I reply.

"It was a lot of work," Chevy says. "I had to put it up before I left to work this morning, and I almost thought it wasn't going to happen. Between the baby and the other kids…it was nuts."

No one asked you to make it, I want to tell her. But instead, I bite my tongue.

"I sent over enough soup to last a few days," Chevy says. "You just need to heat it up. Okay?"

She peers at me, and I nod. Does she think I'm incapable of heating up a pot of soup?

"Why aren't you wearing your uniform?" Chevy asks me, suddenly noticing my gray sweater and black pleated skirt.

"I didn't go to school," I reply shortly.

"Why not? Are you sick?"

"No, I'm not."

Chevy either doesn't notice the terseness of my response or

she chooses to ignore it. "Do you not want to go back because of what happened?" she asks, looking closely at me.

I flush despite myself, and don't answer.

"Hmm," Chevy says, as if thinking to herself. "You know, you can't hide forever. Besides, things blow over. Everyone will forget about this soon enough."

I am silent, still as a statue.

"Don't you think everyone will talk more if you don't go back?" Chevy asks. "I mean, they might assume that something is *really* wrong, *chas v'shalom*. Do you want that?"

I am about to shout at her, to tell her to just go home already, but her words are ringing loudly in my ears. What if... what if she's right?

The thought is disquieting, and I want to put my hands over my ears to drown her out. For the sake of maturity, I busy myself with pouring some of the soup from the container into a pot and setting up the pot on the stovetop.

"Here's chicken and rice," Chevy says, pulling out two foil-wrapped pans. "I made Ima's favorite — barbecue sauce."

"Thanks," I say grudgingly. *She means well*, I tell myself as I turn on the flame beneath the soup pot.

Chevy glances at her watch. "I've got to get home," she says. "I left the kids with a neighbor and told her I'd be back in twenty minutes."

I follow her to the door and watch her run down the walkway to her minivan. It blinks to life and rolls away, down the darkening streets.

I stand at the doorway, my arms wrapped around myself against the frigid air. Then I close the front door gently and go back to the kitchen to check on the soup.

I've got a lot to think about.

Atara

"I NEED A BREAK!" Malkie tells me, grinning impishly.

I'm not amused. Although Malkie's antics usually have me laughing, I'm in no mood for them tonight.

"C'mon, Atara," Malkie cajoles. "We already finished two *perakim*. Can't we take just a teeny-weeny break?"

I wouldn't mind a break myself, but there's no way I want to go downstairs now.

"I'm hungry!" Malkie says, jumping up.

I eye her doubtfully. "We just ate supper half an hour ago."

Malkie clutches her stomach and rolls her eyes dramatically.

"You're the one who should have been in drama, Malkie!" I say, grinning despite myself.

"I'm a growing girl, Atara! I need to eat something. Like you said, supper was already a whole half an hour ago!"

Sighing in exasperation, I stand up.

Malkie peers at me. "Hey, is everything okay? Why so glum tonight?"

I smile automatically, as if everything is perfectly fine. No one — not even my closest friends — will be privy to the knowledge that all is less than perfect in the Gold household.

"Let's go to the kitchen," I say, ignoring her question. I lead the way downstairs, bypassing Elisheva, who is on her way up.

"Guess who's here!" she chirps, her blue eyes sparkling.

"Who?" I ask, my heart sinking.

"Daddy!" She sounds triumphant, as if she's just won a prize. Well, it *is* pretty rare for my sisters to see my father during the week. They're usually fast asleep by the time he gets home.

"And guess who's with him!" Elisheva continues.

"Hmm?" My mouth is suddenly dry.

"That man...um, Mr. Steiner. Right? Was that his name?"

"Something like that," I mutter. The whole situation is so odd. Why is my father home early a second night in a row, and with a guest, no less?

Elisheva continues up the stairs, her ponytail bouncing behind her. I sigh and continue to trudge down, Malkie right behind me.

I am cautious as I step onto the landing. Where are my father and his friend? My head swivels in all directions, until Malkie starts to giggle.

"What are you doing, Atara? Why are you just standing here like that?"

I flush, not sure what to answer. I myself don't know why I'm acting so strangely. There's no real reason to think that anything out of the ordinary is going on in my house...

Except...except for the little clues, scattered here and there.

There's my mother's strained expression, for one. I haven't even heard a word about the Chinese auction leave her lips since last night, which is highly unusual. Then there's my father's behavior around Mr. Steinhaurt. Although I haven't seen them together for more than a few minutes, there was definitely something forced in my father's friendliness. That is so unlike his usual self when he is hosting guests.

A small sigh escapes my lips.

"Atara?" Malkie looks worried now.

I realize that I'd better pull myself together. Perhaps I'm being ridiculous, after all. I do tend to allow my imagination to get the best of me. "Sorry, Malkie, just thinking about something," I tell my friend. "Come, let's go to the kitchen."

In the kitchen, we find Janet busy scrubbing the table to a glossy sheen.

"Janet?" I say. "Do you know where my father is?"

"In the dining room," she replies, jerking her head in the direction of the door adjoining the kitchen. Not surprisingly, that door is now closed.

I'm about to ask where my mother is, when the door opens and my mother comes into the kitchen. She looks surprised to see me.

"We're just taking a short break," I say, suddenly feeling the need to excuse my presence in the kitchen.

My mother nods distractedly as she pulls a pan out of the oven. From the dining room, I can hear the low hum of voices. I toy with saying hello to my father, then decide to wait until later, when he is alone.

I frown. I wonder how long Mr. Steinhaurt will be staying at our house.

I turn to Malkie. "What do you want to eat?" I ask her, opening the pantry. I myself am in no mood for a snack.

Just then, my mother's cell phone, lying on the counter, jangles loudly. "Should I get it?" I offer.

My mother puts the pan down on a towel and shakes her head. "Thanks, I've got it." She glances at the screen and then picks up the phone.

"Hi, Yaffa? Yeah…I know, but I can't really talk right now, okay? …I'll call you back later… Bye…"

My mother sighs as she hangs up, and I know, I just know, that her sigh has nothing to do with the phone call — and everything to do with the man sitting in our dining room right now with my father.

CHAPTER 18

Brachie

It's drizzling, the rain coming down in sporadic spurts, a cold burst of wetness on my hair and face. I can't say I mind. In fact, I'm hoping the shower will turn into a deluge, and that the students of Bais Breindel will be so preoccupied with drying themselves off, that they won't notice when I slink into school like a wanted man avoiding the police.

I sigh heavily, watching the faint puff of air I produce evaporate into the atmosphere. I'm off to school, for better or for worse. And oddly enough, it's Chevy who's behind my decision to rejoin civilization so soon.

After debating her words throughout a sleepless night, I've come to realize that, though I don't like to admit it, my sister is right. Staying home will give gossips more to talk about — and the faster I integrate back into school, as if everything is normal, the sooner this will blow over.

Still, no one said this was going to be easy.

"Hi, Brachie," I hear someone say.

I stick my hands into my pockets, paste a smile on my face, and brace myself. To my surprise, Atara Gold falls into step beside me.

"How are you?" she asks. Then she blushes and falls silent.

Here we go, I tell myself wryly. No doubt Atara wants to hear the latest — how my mother is doing, why she fainted, all the gory details down to their most minute nuances. Well, I'm not going to humor her, of course.

"*Baruch Hashem*," I say, with all the poise I can muster, as if today is just a regular day.

We walk in uncomfortable silence for a few moments. I'm trying to think of something, anything, to say, when Atara speaks up first.

"We missed you at rehearsals," she says. "It was kind of weird for me to read the lines by myself."

I am touched, despite the fact that she's hitting a raw nerve. After all, the reason I missed rehearsals is because of my mother's fainting spell. But neither of us go there.

"Thanks," I say. "When are the next rehearsals?"

"Sunday morning. Ricki and Zehava want us to go through scene two before then."

"We'll have to schedule a practice for one night," I say, and then flush. I sound like I'm so busy, I need a secretary to keep track of my commitments. I want to tell Atara that aside from schoolwork, I'm not *that* busy. True, I've got to keep on top of laundry and basic housework now, but with only three people at home, it's really not a big deal. My sisters are sending over meals, including food for Shabbos, and my mother spends an awful amount of time resting.

The idea of rehearsing in Atara's grand bedroom is actually quite appealing at the moment. I am waiting for Atara to invite me over, but she is quiet.

The rain starts to come down faster, and Atara opens up her umbrella. She holds it over my head as well, and I appreciate the gesture.

"Thanks," I tell her.

That's the last word we exchange as we continue to walk, stepping around puddles and joining the other stragglers heading to school.

Finally, we are almost there, and my heart starts to pound wildly. I look up warily at the huge building looming ahead, and I take a deep breath, trying to steady my jangled nerves.

Then I look up to the overcast, murky sky, knowing that only Hashem can give me the strength to get through this day.

Atara

BRACHIE BODNER IS AMAZING. There's no other way to say it.

I was not at all surprised yesterday when she didn't show up to school. In fact, I hadn't expected to see her in a long time. Even if her mother is fine, the fact remains that Brachie must be feeling humiliated by what happened. That's why I am shocked when I see Brachie strolling to school as if she hasn't a care in the world.

If it were me, *chas v'shalom*, I'd be cowering under my blanket in mortification, wondering what everyone else is whispering about me behind my back. I don't think I'd ever come back to school again. But Brachie is different. She's so strong, so sure of herself...I can't get over it.

For lack of anything else to say, I ask her how she is. What I really want to tell her is that I was thinking of her, and that we were all *davening* for her mother. As it was, though, I think my simple "How are you?" question may actually have offended her — and I'm not sure why.

In any case, I am preoccupied, and it's hard to carry a conversation in that state. Strangely enough, my father was at home this morning when I left the house, and my mother looked tired. Though she mentioned that she was going to run some errands for the auction, I could tell that her heart isn't in it.

And I want to know so badly: what are my parents hiding?!

Though I want desperately to ask them, I'm also too scared to find out the answer... Perhaps this world of insecurity that I currently inhabit is better than the reality may be?

Maybe, or maybe not.

I casually mention rehearsals to Brachie to smooth over the silence between us, but who can think of a play when something terrible might be going on in my very own family? Still, I know that I've got to keep forging onward, if only to keep up my pretense to the rest of the world. Everyone knows that Atara Gold leads the perfect, charmed life, and I'd like to maintain that status quo.

As Brachie and I walk through the wide front doors of Bais Breindel, I assume my ever-present smile, as if I haven't a care in the world. Because, for all intents and purposes, right now I don't.

Brachie

I'm still breathing. It's almost time for recess, and I'm still sitting upright in my chair, surrounded by my classmates. Or maybe, considering what happened to my mother only two days ago, I shouldn't think in those terms…

The main thing is, the situation is not as bad as I envisioned it would be, *baruch Hashem*. Maybe that's because I walked into the classroom with only two minutes to spare before the bell. Things are definitely awkward, to be honest. Girls greet me hesitantly, almost as if they're afraid I'll crumple to the ground as my mother did. It's taking a lot of effort on my part to retain a calm, composed façade, so everyone gets the message that it's time to move on and forget about what happened — as much as possible, at least.

But at least the girls are not whispering behind their hands, as far as I can see. My teachers are treating me normally, too, and I'm glad. By now they've all heard that Mrs. Bodner is bedridden with mono, hardly anything too serious, and the trauma of two mornings ago is receding.

But still. There's no way to stop rumors from taking a flying leap into the realm of the ridiculous. I'm sure by now students around the school have diagnosed my mother with all sorts of horrible things. And I'm sure that my classmates are itching to know what, exactly, transpired that morning — and why I wasn't in school yesterday.

The bell rings for recess, and I shrink back into my seat, trying to make myself invisible. I have no desire to answer any questions, to be the object of everyone's curiosity and the focus of their pity.

I could almost dance with joy when the classroom door opens and Zehava sticks her head inside. "Atara? Brachie?" she says. "Can you come out here for a few minutes?"

I nod, trying not to look too eager. Saved by production!

"Listen," Zehava says urgently when we join her in the hallway. "By Sunday's rehearsal, we really want everyone to know her lines from scenes one and two by heart. Can you two make sure to practice together before then?"

Atara and I nod.

"It's really important," Zehava tells us, looking solemn. "We don't have *that* much time left until production, and we really need to make the most of each rehearsal."

A thrill runs through me. There's a month and a half until the big day, which really isn't a lot of time at all.

"Thanks," Zehava says. She grins. "You guys are great!"

Then she turns and hurries down the hall, no doubt to track down another actress. Atara and I are left facing each other.

"So," I say hesitantly, "when do you want to practice?"

"Tonight is probably okay," Atara says just as uncertainly. "Um…" She thinks, and I wait for her to invite me over. "Could… could we do it at your house?" she finally finishes off, flushing.

I stare at her, not sure what to say. "M-*my* house?" I practically squeak. Since I started high school, no one has ever asked to come to my house.

"Is it okay?" Atara looks nervous. "I know your mother isn't feeling well, but we could stay in your room, right? We wouldn't make too much noise. I just don't know if it's a good night for my parents."

She is rambling, tripping over her words, and I don't know

CURTAIN CALL • 161

what to make of this. Atara is acting so unlike her normal, composed self that I'm confused.

"I don't see why not," I say slowly. "My mother will probably be in her room, anyway. But I'll call her just to make sure it's okay."

Atara looks relieved. "Okay, thanks."

I wonder why she sounds like I'm doing her a favor. Does she *want* to come to Mrs. Bodner's house? It's all so strange that I don't know what to think.

But then my mind flits to the logistics, and I regret ever agreeing to this arrangement. I'm not sure I properly cleaned up before I left to school this morning. What if there are dishes in the sink, or the cushions on the couch aren't perched just so? What if my bed isn't perfectly made or I left something lying around on my desk?

I am fairly cringing with mortification, wondering how the elegant Atara Gold, who resides in a palace, is going to react when she sees my decidedly inelegant house.

"I'll go call my mother now and let her know," Atara tells me.

Wait! I want to call after her. *I changed my mind. This isn't going to work out after all.*

But it's too late.

Atara

AM I CRAZY? Which girl would willingly step into her principal's house just so she could practice some lines? Why couldn't I suggest that Brachie and I practice on the phone?

Of course, I know that we need to work face to face in order to achieve maximum results, but my stomach is twisting, turning, and I can't help wishing I'd just invited Brachie to my own house instead. She's already seen it — she's even met my mother's friends. So what do I have to be embarrassed or nervous about?

I know the answer to that. Our house may be quite different than what Brachie is used to, but that's not what's bothering me right now. My thoughts turn to the mysterious Mr. Steinhaurt and his visits to our house. *He* is the reason why I don't want to bring Brachie home.

Something is going on, and I just don't know what it is. But there's no way I can rehearse with Brachie in my house — not when my mother is walking around with an uptight expression on her face, and not when my father may very well be bringing his new friend home for visit number three. I'm best off at Brachie's house, where I can focus on my lines and try to forget what's going on back at the Gold residence.

Still, I can't help but hope that Mrs. Bodner will stay in her room the whole time. I just wouldn't know what to say to her, especially after what happened during the assembly. The thought of meeting the principal in her house makes me feel so awkward that I squirm right there in my seat as Morah Levine lectures about the *Churban Beis Hamikdash*.

I try to force myself to listen, to take proper notes, but it's no use. All I can think about is going home with Brachie Bodner when school is over for the day.

CHAPTER 19

Brachie

NEVER IN A MILLION YEARS would I have pictured myself doing what I am doing right now. I am heading up the walkway to my house, Atara Gold by my side. We are both quiet, and I wonder if she's nervous to enter her principal's house. It's kind of like entering the lion's lair, isn't it?

Never mind what Atara is feeling; I know that *I* am beside myself with tension! I'm trying to figure out if there's a way to make sure the house is presentable before Atara gets a good look around. Maybe I'll seat her in my room and then go downstairs to get us some snacks. I could take the opportunity to dash around the house, straighten up here and there, put away anything that's out of place. Or maybe I could —

I blink, bewildered, as the front door is pulled open before I can even fumble for my key.

"Wh-what?" I splutter. Standing before me are Dassi's little girls. "Tova! Zeesy! What are you doing here?"

Dassi comes up behind them, her snood slightly askew. "Tova and Zeesy are being *so* quiet, so Bubby can rest, right?" she whispers loudly. She smiles broadly at me. "Hi, Brachie. We're here getting supper ready for you."

My heart is sinking deeper than the *Titanic*. The situation is slipping out of my control faster than I'd thought possible — and I realize that I never had any control of it to begin with.

"Y-you cooked supper here?" I ask, wondering how I'll be able to clean up the kitchen before Atara gets a good view of it.

Dassi shakes her head. "Nope, we're just warming it up." She moves back so we can enter the house, and she peers at Atara. "You look familiar... Oh! Aren't you —"

"Miri's sister," Atara finishes, grinning.

For once, I am grateful for the dim lighting in the front hallway. My cheeks are flaming, burning hot, and I wish I could just bolt up to my room and lock the door behind me.

How utterly embarrassing! No doubt Atara is remembering Dassi's messy apartment, the things strewn all over the place, and the piles of stuff on every spare surface. I cough, hoping I still can salvage the situation, somehow.

And then I see it. Behind Dassi, the living room looks like a storm — or rather, Dassi's lively brood — has ripped through it. Yechiel is having a heyday while his mother's back is turned, upending anything and everything in sight. Books, newspapers, and the toys my mother keeps in a corner for the grandchildren are all over the place. The couch cushions are likewise strewn all over the floor, evidence to a lively game of leap frog that must have gone on there.

I stand there, my mouth agape and my head hammering.

"Are you okay, Brachie?" Dassi asks me, finally realizing that I am focusing only on the area beyond her right shoulder.

I open and close my mouth wordlessly, yet no sound emerges.

"Oh, my!" Atara cries. She runs toward Yechiel before he manages to pull the tablecloth off of the dining room table.

I flex and un-flex my fingers, not believing this is really happening. My mind sweeps me back to a few nights before, when I entered the Golds' pristine, palatial residence. Forget the fact that our furniture is somewhat outdated and our kitchen could use a facelift. As long as our house looks neat and presentable, I can handle that. But this…this disaster? It's absolutely unthinkable!

All at once, I'm filled with rage toward Dassi, my oldest sister whom I've always adored. I can no longer focus on her sunny disposition, laidback friendliness, and all-encompassing warmth. I want to confront her, demand to know how she can be such a slob — but I hold myself back. The fireworks will have to wait until Atara Gold leaves the house.

I turn to Dassi, forcing a stiff smile to my lips. "How…nice," I manage to say. "I'm so…um…happy your children had such a good time here. But maybe they could clean up now?"

Dassi is looking at me strangely, and I feel a queer sensation lodge itself in my chest. Dassi would do anything for me, and I know it. She's fiercely loyal to her family and, of all my sisters, is always there at our beck and call, despite her growing family.

But with all that, I can't help but harden my heart now. The mess in our house is simply inexcusable. I'll never be able to live this down.

"Shall we go upstairs?" I say politely to Atara. She nods just as politely, and I wish, wish, wish I could know what she's thinking. Or maybe it's better not to know.

For good measure, I turn to Dassi's girls. "You're both going to clean up Bubby's house very nicely, right?" I say to them. "You know Bubby doesn't like a mess."

I toss my head in Dassi's general direction but avoid looking at her directly. "Thanks for supper," I say.

Then I flee upstairs, making sure that I can't see the inevitable hurt in my sister's eyes.

Atara

THE ONLY THING I CAN THINK as I head up the stairs with Brachie, is how wonderful her family is. It's so touching that her big sister is downstairs, making sure that Brachie and her parents have a hot meal for supper. Mrs. Fleishman's children — although they're adorable — sure look like a handful, and it can't be easy for her to bring everyone over at this time of day. Still, she dropped all of her other obligations to come and help out her mother. I wonder if Brachie appreciates what she has.

Brachie turns to me as we step onto the landing. "We have to be really quiet now," she whispers. "We're going to pass my mother's room."

My stomach lurches. How strange to be tiptoeing past Mrs. Bodner's bedroom. Actually, it's weird just to be in her house.

I look around me with interest. Family pictures adorn the walls of the hallway, and a small light fixture emits a soft glow. The whole house seems warm and cozy. I can't help contrasting it with my own picture-perfect house, where nothing is ever out of place and Janet walks around *shpritzing* everything to a shiny sheen...

Brachie leads me into her room. She looks uncomfortable, and I wonder why. Maybe it's because her room is functional and practical, with its sturdy brown furniture and simple bedspread, so unlike my own luxurious, lavender habitat. Still, there are pretty knickknacks placed in strategic locations around the room, and nice posters with inspiring sayings adorn the walls. It's a pleasant room, and I'm wondering if I should tell her so.

But just then, Brachie speaks up. "So, should we begin?" she asks, without preamble.

I nod, and try to lose myself in the script. Right now, we are Juanita and Maria, two conniving servants plotting the downfall of the family who has employed us and trusted us. We scheme and plot together, ever mindful to keep our voices down so as not to disturb Mrs. Bodner. We make a pretty good team, if I do say so myself.

I feel myself being lured into the plot, and I can tell Brachie feels the same way. When we read our lines together, we are suddenly *there* — in Spain, in the sprawling estate whose stunning exterior belies the evil lurking within.

"You know," Brachie says, looking up suddenly from her script, "isn't it scary how easily we *become* Maria and Juanita? Like, we pretend to be them and feel like them and think like them...and suddenly we *are* them!"

"I know what you mean," I reply. "But that's what acting is all about — becoming your character."

"Still," Brachie says slowly, "it just goes to show how easily a person can adapt behaviors or ways of thinking that he never thought he would."

I look at her, impressed. She's Mrs. Bodner's daughter, through and through. I'm not sure if Brachie would appreciate my saying so, though, so I keep that thought to myself.

I catch sight of my watch. "Wow, it got late," I say, surprised that I feel disappointed. "I told my mother I'd be home by six."

Brachie walks me downstairs. I look around for Mrs. Fleishman and her kids, but it's quiet. "Your sister left?" I ask.

Brachie nods, and there's a strange expression on her face.

"Oh, well," I say. "I wanted to say goodbye to her. She's really special, your sister. And it must be so nice for you to have your sister's kids around."

This time, there's no mistaking the expression on Brachie's face. She's clearly taken aback.

"Yeah," she murmurs, almost as if to herself. She shows me to the door.

"Thanks," I say.

Brachie smiles at me, and her face lights up. "Thanks for coming," she replies.

I leave the house, my knapsack hoisted on my back. The wind whips my face, and I trudge through the darkening evening toward my own house.

Brachie

SHE'S REALLY SPECIAL, *your sister. She's really special.*

Atara's words swirl around in my head as I serve my mother supper at the kitchen table.

I *know* Dassi's special. I don't need Atara to tell me that. So why do I feel like I just found out something I never knew before?

I set my mother's plate before her with more force than I intended, and some sauce splashes onto the tablecloth.

"Oops," I say, hurrying to get a napkin. "Sorry."

"How'd it go tonight with Atara?" my mother asks me as I soak up the gravy.

"It went well," I reply. "It's funny, but we really do work well together."

My mother smiles and winks. "I heard you two coming up the stairs, but I figured it would be best if I stay in my room."

I sit down across from my mother. "Thanks," I say gratefully.

My mother looks down at her robe. "Well, I couldn't exactly have a student see me like this, could I?"

She laughs and I join in, feeling lighter than I've felt in ages. It's funny, but now that my mother is home sick, I'm spending more time with her than I ever used to. In school I would see her in passing, in the halls, during assemblies — but she was always Mrs. Bodner, the principal, and I didn't want to emphasize my relationship with her. But now, at home, we're both unwinding in ways that we never have before.

There's silence as we chew our chicken cutlets and mashed potatoes. Dassi is a great cook, and I hadn't realized how hungry I am.

I'm just about to ask my mother if she wants some more, when the phone rings. "I'll get it," I say.

I glance at the caller ID screen, and my insides knot together. *Fleishman, Shimon.* I'm about to hand the phone to my mother, when, on impulse, I decide to answer it instead.

"Hi, Dassi," I say as I bring my plate to the counter.

"Hi, Brachie," my sister says with her customary warmth.

"I-I wanted to thank you," I say, stumbling over my words. "For supper. And for...everything."

"You're welcome," Dassi replies, and I can tell that she's accepted my unspoken apology.

"Here's Ima," I say, handing the phone to my mother.

I sit back down at the table as my mother lapses into a conversation with Dassi. It really wasn't hard to make amends with my sister, I realize. I can't remember ever getting upset at Dassi before, actually — and I'm embarrassed that I felt ashamed of my well-meaning sister.

Then my thoughts turn to my next sister in line, Chevy, and my stomach clenches. I fiddle with my fork, wondering why just a minute ago I was in the mood for seconds. Now I suddenly feel very full.

Images of Chevy ordering me around, assuming that I'm always available, at her constant beck and call, parade through my mind. Somehow, I don't think I can ever summon the strength to set things straight with her.

Atara

"YOU MUST SEE what I picked up today, Atara!"

My mother is animated, smiling, as she leads me to the den. This room has become her unofficial Chinese auction meeting place. In the corner, there's a neat stack of items she and her friends have picked up already, and it's steadily growing by the day.

"Look!" my mother tells me. She riffles through a large shopping bag and pulls out long, elegant candles in a light shade of green. "These are an *exact* match for the tablecloths Mrs. Cohen found!" my mother gushes.

I smile as I watch my mother in action, but I'm puzzled. The tension that's been clinging to her like lint to a woolen skirt seems to have dissipated, just as suddenly as it came. I wonder if I've simply imagined the strain of the past few days.

I toy with asking my mother if everything is okay, but I don't want to dispel the carefree expression on her face. Besides, she'd probably call me her drama queen and tell me that not all situations call for theatrics.

Esti runs into the den, her blonde braid flying behind her. "Mommy!" she cries, holding tight to my mother's legs.

My mother tries to extricate herself. "Careful, Esti," she says. "Let me put these candles back in the bag. I don't want them to break."

"But I don't want you to leave me!" Esti wails.

My mother looks down at her, frowning slightly. "I'm not leaving you, Esti. Why would you say that I am?"

"Elisheva said!" Esti pouts. "She said Daddy's going to a place called Parry and you're going with him, and maybe this time you won't come home."

I take the candles from my mother's hands so she can deal with Esti.

"Of course that's not true," my mother says soothingly. She leads Esti to the couch and pulls her onto her lap. "Did Daddy and I come back the last time we went away?"

Esti nods. "But it was so long!" she complains. "And now

you're going to Parry."

"Only Daddy's going to Paris," I tell her.

"Actually," my mother says slowly, "Daddy's not going to France in the end."

"Really?" The word bursts out of me excitedly, although I notice that my mother doesn't look too happy. "Why not?"

"It's not...it's not working out," my mother says delicately. I can tell she doesn't want to say anything more, and I don't press her. But I'm concerned. My father's business is contingent on his startups in other companies. If this trip is canceled, something must be very wrong.

Immediately, I realize what the problem must be. My father's business must be going under!

I stand there, frozen, images of *tzedakah* organizations' boxes filled with food, in front of our elegant front door, bombarding my mind. But wait — if we're losing all of our money, we'll probably have to move away from our beautiful house, too! My mind is immediately overtaken with pictures of how our rundown hovel will look.

I swallow, hard. For all that our lives have changed since my father's corporation took off, I've gotten used to the many extra frills — and I don't think I could manage without them.

Then I realize: This is not at all about the extras. We'll probably have to give up everything — everything!

I imagine our family, stuffed into a cramped apartment whose walls are cracked and peeling. My designer clothes will be replaced with raggedy hand-me-downs culled from crowded thrift stores. I will be a social pariah, a total outcast. Will my friends ever talk to me again? Look at me again? Will

I lose my entire standing in society once our family loses our economic status?

I can hear, as if from a distance, the growl of the vacuum cleaner as it comes to life. I wonder fleetingly where Janet will find employment, then shove her out of my mind. She's the *least* of my concerns right now!

My mother doesn't notice my stricken face, how my thoughts are colliding and crashing in my brain so that I can't even form a single coherent word. Instead, she's still focused on Esti.

"Do you want to come shopping with me tomorrow after school?" my mother asks Esti. "We need to buy you new shoes."

Esti's eyes light up, and I stare at both of them. If my mother is buying new shoes, things can't be that bad, can they? Or maybe she just wants to keep up a façade for the world — and for us, her family?

I look more closely at my mother. She doesn't look like a woman whose entire world is about to cave in on her. In fact, she looks pretty calm as she sits on the couch with Esti.

And me? I'm thoroughly, utterly confused. Are my assumptions right or wrong? Are things just fine with my family…or far from it? I toy with the idea of calling one of the Big Three to distract me from my tumultuous thoughts, then nix the idea the next second. I'm in no mood for any of my friends' bubbly chatter right now.

I wish there were someone else I could turn to, someone who would understand the thoughts rattling in my brain, someone who could help me make sense of everything in my head. For all that I'm regarded as a popular, sought-after girl in my school, right now I'm feeling lonelier than I've ever felt before.

CHAPTER 20

Brachie

It's strange, but sometimes when you finally get what you wanted so badly, you realize that you never really wanted it to begin with.

The candles flicker on the dining room table, casting shadows on the walls beside them. They look oddly lonely tonight, without any of my sisters' flames beside them. My sisters have agreed that until my mother recovers, my home will remain off-limits for Shabbos visits.

This is what I always wanted, right? Some peace and quiet, a chance to rest up from the hectic week without little kids crying, fussing, and wreaking havoc all over the place… And yet…I find that I miss all that.

"It's quiet, isn't it?" My mother speaks up from the armchair where she's resting.

"Yeah," I agree. "It's weird."

"But nice," my mother says, to my surprise.

I look at her. "But…I thought you like when everyone comes over. Aren't you lonely without them?"

This time it's my mother's turn to be surprised. "Lonely? I have *you* here, don't I?"

I squirm. "Yeah, but…I don't know. I thought you missed all the noise in the house, and that's why you always like to have the married kids over."

My mother looks thoughtful. "I wouldn't say I miss the noise, per se. I do enjoy having my children over, of course… but I don't feel a void, or anything like that, if that's what you mean."

"Empty nest syndrome," I murmur.

I'm embarrassed when my mother overhears me. "My nest isn't empty, Brachie," she counters. "I still have the boys to marry off, even if they are away at yeshivah, and there's you at home. Where did you get such an idea?"

I spread out my hands, as if groping for an answer. "I don't know," I say hesitantly. "You're so happy when everyone's over…"

"And you're not?"

I'm not sure if my mother means that as a question or a statement. "Um… Well, I…" I fall silent, not sure how to say what I really mean. My mother is looking at me patiently, and I forge on, reassured. "I mean…I like when everyone comes to visit. Their kids are cute, and it's nice, but…but I don't like when they expect me to pick up after them. It's like they think I'm their personal nanny sometimes."

My mother is silent, and I'm nervous that I've offended her somehow. Then she looks at me. "I hear what you're saying,

Brachie. And I can try to speak to your sisters for you, if you'd like, to let them know how you feel. But it might be easier if you understand where they're coming from, too. They work hard and have so little time to relax. I don't think they realize that you also need your own down time. Of course they need to be made aware of that and of how you feel, but my point is, no one is trying to take advantage of you, or anything like that."

I snuggle deeper into the couch, mulling over my mother's words. I'd never thought about it like that before.

"I don't know," I say doubtfully. "I don't mind helping them out — at least some of them. I *want* to help them — and their kids are so cute! But I just don't want to be treated like a slave, you know what I mean?"

I can tell that my mother knows exactly what I mean. She's about to answer me when we hear my father knock on the front door, before he pushes it open.

"We'll finish this conversation another time, okay?" my mother tells me. She smiles at me, and I smile back. We haven't really reached any concrete solutions to the problem, but just releasing some of my frustration has helped me feel so much better.

"Good Shabbos!" my father greets us as he enters the room.

"Good Shabbos," my mother and I reply.

I stand up and head to the kitchen to bring the wine to the table. It's funny, I muse as I open the refrigerator, but if I'd known last week what this week would bring, I'd never have thought I had the strength to get through it. But now, with everything that has happened — *despite* everything that happened, and maybe even because of it — I'm feeling stronger somehow, and more optimistic than I've felt in a long time.

Atara

I'M IN NO MOOD to make small talk with Tziri Cohen as we head toward my dining room. After a long week, I'm tired, and I wish we weren't entertaining the Cohen family tonight during our *seudah*.

I'm quiet as my mother and Mrs. Cohen decide where Tziri's younger siblings should sit. Bashie Cohen ends up sandwiched between Elisheva and Esti, and Dini Cohen is right next to Miri. Everyone is finally satisfied with the seating arrangements, and we are able to commence with our *seudah*.

I eye my father as he sings "Shalom Aleichem" with Mr. Cohen and his sons. He seems relaxed and upbeat to me, and I wonder if it's just a show or if everything really is perfectly fine. Then again, my father makes an effort every week to shove business concerns out of his consciousness come Shabbos. At our Shabbos table, talk of work and finances is strictly avoided. So the fact that he seems calm now is not really an indication that everything is okay.

I glance at my mother. She's smiling, playing the role of the gracious hostess. There's absolutely no sign of the stress I saw on her during the week.

I half-close my eyes, trying to let the serenity of Shabbos settle over me, too. There's no need to worry today, I tell myself. Shabbos is here.

As the *seudah* wears on, the conversation at the table veers into predictable directions. My father is busy discussing a new *sefer* with Mr. Cohen, while my mother chats with Mrs. Cohen. The younger kids are busy shmoozing with each other — and I'm left to engage in conversation with Tziri.

I try to keep my mind focused, but it's drifting all over the place. The past week has been just so long and draining and —

"Do you know what I mean? Uh…Atara?" Tziri is giving me a funny look, and I snap to attention.

"Sorry," I say, somewhat lamely. "I'm just so exhausted. What were you saying?"

Immediately, Tziri's eyes shine with admiration. "Yeah, you must be really tired," she says. "You have a major part in drama."

I flush under the hero-worship of her gaze. "Well…"

Elisheva picks up the thread of our conversation. "Atara is the best actress!" she puts in proudly.

My mother beams at me across the table, then turns to Mrs. Cohen. "Production time is always so hectic," she says. "It's really something to get used to!"

Tziri's younger sisters start to bombard me with questions about the play and my role. I am thrust into the limelight as I tell them the backdrop of *With Hearts of Fire*, and I am suddenly enjoying myself.

"Maybe next year I'll try out for drama," Tziri says wistfully.

I smile benevolently at her. "It definitely doesn't hurt to try," I tell her. "And it's so much fun!"

It really is, I realize, as I reflect on my rehearsals with Brachie. It's fun to adopt a character so different from your own personality…and it's nice to get to know another girl in a way you've never known her before.

Tziri peppers me with more questions. Clearly, in her mind, drama is all about glamour and excitement. But by now I know that it's also a whole lot of hard work, as is anything that you want to see results from. And there's still a long haul in front of me before the big day arrives.

Still, I can't say I mind the admiring glances coming my way. And as Janet brings in an array of kugels on a crystal platter, I am aware of only one thing: keeping up the pretense that Atara Gold leads the perfect existence.

Brachie

I FEEL FUNNY WALKING ALONE, especially as I pass groups of chattering, laughing girls of all ages and stages. I always get the feeling that lone people are frowned upon by social butterflies — even if I do happen to enjoy my own company.

Still, even if I *were* looking for a companion, whom exactly should I walk together with?

I pass yet another group of teenage girls who look about my age. I don't know them, and they don't know me; I stride quickly past them with a polite "good Shabbos." I'm on a mission, after all: to visit Dassi. I know my big sister will accept my company with her wide, easy smile, and I want to show her how sorry I am for the way I acted when I brought Atara Gold home.

Dassi's big heart is ever-accepting of everyone she knows, with all their faults...and I wish I could say the same of myself. I know I'm lucky to have a sister like Dassi, and I hope my visit tells her what I'm way too shy to say.

I pass by the park, filled with happy, squealing children and chattering mothers. It's a beautiful day, unseasonably warm, and many families are out in full force. I am walking by the park's entrance when I see a familiar green-and-navy coat, with a cute, chubby face perched atop it.

No. It can't be.

I squint, sure my eyes are deceiving me.

"Brachie! What are you doing here?"

I recoil as a most familiar voice assaults my ears. I want to pretend I didn't hear anything and keep right on walking, but instead I do the mature — and appropriate — thing: I look at my sister and paste a polite smile on my face. "Good Shabbos, Chevy. How are you?"

Chevy looks slightly frazzled as she jiggles her crying baby in her arms. "Wonderful, *baruch Hashem*," she says distractedly. "Where are you going? Why are you alone?"

At that, I almost walk away. Did she *need* to highlight my status as a loner? I decide not to answer her question. Instead, I aim my own at her. "What are *you* doing here?"

Oops. I hope Chevy doesn't pick up the hostility in my tone.

"We're by my sister-in-law for Shabbos...you know, Sheva, the one who moved here about half a year ago. We've never gone to her for Shabbos, but...there's a first for everything, right?" Chevy ends off lightly enough, but I can see that she looks strained. I wonder if her visit is proceeding as she would have liked.

"Why didn't you come visit if you're staying so close by?" I ask. I'm secretly relieved she didn't, but it's not like Chevy to avoid a visit with my parents when she's in the area.

"Sima woke up not feeling well today," Chevy says, glancing anxiously at her little daughter. "I didn't think it would be a good idea to expose Ima to whatever she might have."

I peer at my niece. She looks wan and vulnerable, and I want to give her a hug. "So why are you shlepping her outside?" I ask.

Chevy looks upset, and I wish I could bite back the question. "She keeps kvetching and crying, and the baby is teething and miserable, too." Chevy sighs. "My sister-in-law always naps on Shabbos, and I really didn't want to make her miss that. She works so hard all week, and I would feel awful if she couldn't sleep because of my kids' crying…"

I nod, suddenly understanding. Poor Chevy, stuck for Shabbos with two fretful children, in a house where she doesn't feel fully comfortable. I can't help but feel bad for her. "Why don't I help you?" I offer spontaneously, holding out my hands to the baby.

Chevy is clearly stunned by my offer. "Are…are you sure?" she asks, still holding on to her baby.

I nod. "I'm positive."

"Aren't you on your way somewhere?"

I look at Chevy, noticing the dark circles under her eyes. "Not really," I tell her. After all, I was on the way to help my sister — and right now, I'm doing just that.

I take the baby into my arms and find a spot on a nearby bench. Chevy pulls Sima onto her lap and waves to Shimmy, who is running to the top of a slide.

We sit silently, my sister and I, as the world continues to

carry on. And I can't help wondering: *whatever is going on in my sister's mind?*

Atara

SECRETS, SECRETS. The Gold house can't possibly hold any more secrets in it. Maybe that's why my parents are outside right now, strolling around the gorgeous grounds of our house. My father looks serious, and I can tell my mother isn't talking much.

I can't remember the last time they walked aimlessly around the yard. When they do go on walks, it's down a few blocks, maybe even more than a few blocks. But just around the house? Weird.

I drum my fingers on the cold pane, smudging up the glass but knowing that Janet will no doubt come around later tonight or tomorrow to rub away any tell-tale fingerprints. Why, I wonder, would my parents want to stay close to our house?

And then it hits me, like a hardball I can't manage to catch in time. Obviously, my parents don't want to meet other people on the street — and that can't be a good thing. My suspicions from a few nights before rear their ugly head.

We're going to be reduced to poverty.

My heart sinks, even as my mind tells me that something isn't adding up. If the situation were that drastic, how could my parents have entertained the Cohens with such ease only the night before? And why haven't they fired Janet yet? In all the books I've read, when families had to cut back on expenses, the maid was the first to go.

So maybe it's something else, then.

I jump up and pace the lavender carpet of my room. The décor is fit for a princess, as my mother fondly told me when we decorated the room. But right now, I don't feel like a princess; I feel more like a prisoner.

A prisoner.

I pause in my tracks as my eyes widen in horror. That's it, isn't it? My father is going to jail!

My parents are not there to confirm the awful truth, but I can feel it in my bones. That man — Mr. Steinhaurt — is somehow wrapped up in the whole business. Maybe he was blackmailing my father...or maybe he tricked him... Right now, it doesn't matter. What *can* matter, when the life I've known is about to dissolve into millions of tiny, sharp shards?

I narrow my eyes thoughtfully. Something still doesn't make sense. Why would my parents entertain the Cohens with this awful shadow of...of a *prison sentence* hanging over our heads?

I shake my head. How can I know why they chose to invite the Cohens for Shabbos this week? Maybe they'd invited them weeks ago and couldn't back out now. They wouldn't want the Cohens to suspect anything, of course.

I resume my frantic pacing again. The Cohens might not suspect anything right now, but they'll know soon enough. The whole world will know!

The bitter realization that I may be about to become the town's newest *nebbach* case and piece of gossip makes me feel sick. I sink onto my bed, feeling waves of nausea rock me. *What in the world am I going to do about this?*

I sit up suddenly, and my head spins. Forget about me, I tell myself. It's my father who's going to sit in jail. What's *he* going to do about this?

I jump to my feet and find myself back at the window, watching my parents. My mother looks up suddenly and, catching sight of me, waves. I shrink back and pick up my arm weakly, feeling as if I've just been caught eavesdropping…or spying. I blush. What is *wrong* with me?

I peek down at my parents again. My mother is looking somewhere in the distance and shading her eyes. My father is laughing. They don't look like two people with the weight of the world on their shoulders.

I drum my fingernails on the pane again, wondering if my imagination has run a few blocks ahead of me. The conclusions I've jumped to are laughable, really. But I can't help wondering…is there some truth to any of them?

For one crazy moment, I feel like flying downstairs and asking my parents if any of my guesses are right. And if they're not, if someone could please tell me what *is* going on. But the next moment, I feel weak with worry. If something really is terribly wrong, there's no way I'll be able to handle it. So maybe I don't really want to know what's happening…

And so I continue to stare out the window, feeling miserable, worried, and alone.

CHAPTER 21

Brachie

WHAT TO WEAR? What to wear?

I stand in front of my closet, still clad in my nightgown. The clock on my night table is steadily ticking away the minutes, and still, I'm no closer to coming to a decision. The green sweater or the turquoise top? The black skirt or the gray one with the wide pleats?

The knowledge that the glamorous Atara Gold will be standing beside me almost the whole time only makes my decision harder. The last thing I want is to feel like an outdated *shlump* beside her up-to-date, expensive ensemble.

I need something nice — very nice — but also something that is befitting of The Principal's Daughter. The knowledge that, as a Bodner, I am constantly on display, is like a crushing burden right now. If I find it hard to be under constant scrutiny when I'm wearing my uniform, how am I supposed to feel when attired in regular clothing of my own choice?

This is getting ridiculous, and I know it. When rehearsals were scheduled for Sunday morning, it wasn't so that I could waste an hour in front of my closet, pondering what to wear. Still, how am I supposed to even think of rehearsing when I have no suitable clothing for the occasion?

I fold my arms and tap my foot, thinking quickly. There's no point in riffling through my drawers for the umpteenth time — I know exactly what's inside each of them. I'm waiting for a miracle — for the outfit of my dreams to appear magically in my closet. But waiting for my dream to materialize will only result in me missing the rehearsal. And the heads are required to take attendance at each rehearsal; too many missed ones and we face being thrown out of production.

I sigh. How pathetic — to miss a rehearsal because of a deficient wardrobe! Besides, it seems that rehearsals will be scheduled for every Sunday from now until production, and I can't exactly miss those rehearsals each week because I have nothing to wear.

Resignedly, I reach into a drawer and pull out my trusty navy sweater. Shifra always says that you can't go wrong with classic, and for now I'll fall back on her advice. I choose a pleated black skirt to go along with it — and the die has been cast. In these clothes I will head off to Bais Breindel for the morning, for better or for worse.

Within moments I'm dressed and heading downstairs. After *davening* and a quick breakfast, I zip into my coat, call goodbye to my parents, and walk quickly toward school.

From a distance I can see Atara Gold, turning onto the block of Bais Breindel. The knowledge that whatever she's wearing will be absolutely dazzling, with a designer label, does not make me feel very good. I try to tell myself that I don't care, that it's just clothes, that I look perfectly presentable and put-together.

But for all of my mental pep talk, I *do* care.

Atara

I DON'T THINK I can handle Sunday morning rehearsals.

The knowledge that in just under an hour, I — or, to be more precise, my clothing — will be under the scrutiny of a school-full of girls, does not excite me in the least bit. In fact, it makes me want to crawl right back under my warm down blanket. Which is kind of funny, considering that my family might be in real trouble. What are clothes and fashion statements compared to whatever crisis is looming over us?

But strangely, right now I'm focusing on one thing only: playing the part of Atara Gold — a good girl from a well-to-do family. Somehow, in the morning sunshine, yesterday's fears are just that — fears. I can tell myself, at least for now, that everything is okay. Because at the moment, it is. Isn't it?

And so I stand in front of my closet, which stretches along the entire length of one wall. The array of choices does not make my decision any easier.

Should I wear the purple sweater or the light-gray pullover? How about the new pink top that perfectly suits my complexion...or what about the mint-green zip-up that makes my eyes shine like emeralds?

I dismiss outfit after outfit. Some are too dressy; others are too plain. Some are going out of style, while others are way too trendy for a regular Sunday morning. I need to dress to impress, while not being too over-the-top.

Striking the right balance is harder than I thought it would be, and suddenly I think of Brachie Bodner. Brachie is beyond caring about her clothes, and I feel ashamed. She would never stand in front of her closet like me, discarding outfit after outfit while she tries to figure out how to wow all the girls of Bais Breindel.

I feel petty, pathetic, as I finger yet another skirt. As a Gold, I know my wardrobe will be under intense scrutiny by all the fashion-savvy students in my school. Of course, the contents of my closet would pass the most rigorous of fashion standards — but suddenly I'm wary of wearing anything that reeks of an expensive price tag, something that would cause Brachie to look down on me. I decide to choose something sensible and refined, something I can feel good in, without second-guessing myself, when I'm standing beside Brachie.

Half an hour later, I'm ready to go. "Bye," I call to my mother and sisters, who are seated in the kitchen.

My mother looks relaxed in a burgundy pre-tied snood, her hands cupped around her favorite mug. She is laughing at something that Miri is saying, and I pause. Is everything okay...or isn't it? Would my mother be laughing like this if there really is a problem?

I sigh. I can't make heads or tails of what's going on.

"Leaving, Tari?" my mother says, looking up.

I nod.

My mother smiles. "Good luck!"

"Thanks," I reply, turning away from the sun-dappled kitchen.

Maybe I've been busy jumping to conclusions. Or maybe I haven't been. There's no way to know. But I do know one thing: I've got to hurry if I want to make it to rehearsal on time.

After a brisk walk, I step through the front door of Bais Breindel, feeling somewhat self-conscious. Girls are scattered all over, talking, exchanging hellos…and ever so casually looking each other up and down. Ugh.

I hurry to the classroom where drama practices will be held, keeping my coat zippered. I paste my confident smile on my face, nodding at classmates as I pass them in the hall.

"Hi," Ricki and Zehava say to me as I enter the classroom.

I smile at them as well while I take a seat at the side of the room. Brachie walks in a few moments after me, looking flushed from the cold. She opens her coat before sitting down next to me…and my eyes widen.

At first, I'm mortified. This has never before happened to me, fashion-conscious Atara Gold. But suddenly, the irony of the situation hits me, and I have a crazy desire to laugh out loud.

I unzip my own coat, grinning. Brachie catches my eye as she sees what I'm wearing, and then we both start to giggle. In our navy sweaters and black skirts, Brachie and I are… matching.

Brachie

"Juanita, this is it!" I cry, my eyes darting in all directions. "This is the moment we've been waiting for."

Juanita's eyes overwhelm her face as she whispers tremulously, "Yes?"

"One minute, Atara," Ricki cuts in. "You need to remember to face the audience the whole time. It's your facial expression that counts the most in this scene, not what you say, and we lose that when you turn to Brachie."

"Okay," Atara says good-naturedly. She turns to face the "audience" — a row of chairs set up in the back of the classroom — and gives a mock bow. All three of us burst out laughing.

I smooth my pleated skirt and glance down at my script. I'm amazed at how comfortable I feel, closeted in a room with only Ricki and Atara.

"This scene is major," Ricki tells us, as if we didn't know that ourselves. Just the fact that she's rehearsing it with us over and over again is revealing enough. "Besides for setting the atmosphere of the entire play — making the audience feel afraid and anxious to know what's coming next — this is going to lead to the action in the next scene, when Don and Dona Mendeles are arrested."

I can't resist exchanging a grin with Atara. Ricki is only two years older than us, but she sounds like she's reading her lines straight out of a book.

"Okay," Ricki says, glancing down at the sheaf of papers in her hand. "Brachie, let's start over again — facing the 'audience' the whole time. You can look at each other when you're supposed to, of course — but only say your lines when the audience can see your face."

Atara and I exchange another grin before turning to Ricki, mock-solemn expressions on our faces.

"Great," Ricki tells us, seeing that we mean business. "Let's get started, then."

"Juanita!" I say again. "This is it! This is the moment we've been waiting for."

Atara fairly quivers with excitement, and I'm impressed by her acting abilities. "Yes?" she whispers, making sure she faces the chairs.

Ricki nods in approval and motions for me to go on. I try not to look down at my script, although Ricki is permitting us to use them for this rehearsal.

"The salt," I say, checking to make sure no one is around. "The cook was using salt today while preparing the meat for dinner."

"So what?" Atara bursts out impatiently.

My eyes gleam, or at least I hope they do. "Patience, Juanita," I say. "Don't Jews use salt to make meat permissible for them to eat?"

"What of it?" Atara says, folding her arms.

We've decided, Atara and I, that I will be the clever maid, while Atara will be slower and inadvertently mess things up. Ricki and Zehava loved our idea and helped us revise some lines. I think the audience will get a kick out of our roles as well.

"Well," I say, my tone sinister, "if the Don and Dona are salting their meat, then perhaps...perhaps they are secret Jews!"

Atara jumps back, her eyes wide. "Secret Jews! Why, we must inform on them immediately!"

"Hush!" I chasten her. "Patience, patience. We must collect evidence, slowly, slowly, build our case…until the facts stare at them in the face and they will have no choice but to confess."

Atara is about to answer when the door swings open and Zehava walks in. "Sorry to interrupt," she says, glancing at me and Atara. "Ricki, can you help me out in the other room for a few minutes?"

"Yeah." Ricki looks back at us. "You two keep practicing here, okay? I'll be back soon."

The door is still ajar when I make out Rena Hoch striding past our room, laughing loudly with Nechie Bookman.

"Such fun!" Rena is saying. "No teachers, no Mrs. Bodner bossing us around! I wish school was like this every day!" She chortles and disappears from sight, but I can still hear her laughter wafting down the hall.

She doesn't mean anything by that, and I know it…but I can't help feeling hurt. I'm too sensitive, perhaps, but the comment still stings. Why, oh, why, can't Rena ever keep her thoughts to herself?

I sigh as I look down at the slightly dog-eared script I'm holding. The high I've been feeling during this rehearsal evaporates, and try as I might, I just can't recapture it.

Atara

"Where were we?" I say to Brachie. It's hard to pick up our lines from before Zehava burst into the room.

"Um…" Brachie riffles through her script, her shoulders drooping slightly.

"Oh, here!" I say, finding the place. "We're on the top of page thirteen. Okay, here goes… Maria, how can we know if the meat has been salted?"

Brachie sighs. "I told you already — we have to keep our eyes open, be patient."

I look at Brachie, wondering what's come over her. The words re lackluster, uttered without any emotion whatsoever.

"Well," I say, resuming my next line, "what if we don't find any other evidence? What if —"

I pause. Brachie is supposed to cut me off, and she totally missed her cue. In fact, she's not even listening to me. She looks upset, and I wonder what could have happened to effect such a swift change of mood.

I quickly run through the events of the last few minutes — Zehava's interruption, Ricki's brief exit…and Rena Hoch's passing comment.

Suddenly, I understand what this is all about. Poor Brachie. I never really thought about what it must be like for her to have her mother so much in the forefront of Bais Breindel's existence.

"Brachie?" I say softly.

She glances up, sighing slightly.

"It's okay," I tell her.

She looks at me, puzzled. I'm not sure if I should say anything or just push the whole thing under the tiled floor, but I forge on.

"Don't pay attention to what other girls say," I continue, feeling slightly foolish. Here I am, Atara Gold, a girl who cares very much about public opinion, and I'm telling Brachie Bodner how she should react to an insensitive comment.

I flinch, not sure how Brachie will take to my words. I peek at her...and am relieved to see that she's not upset. In fact, she looks somewhat mollified.

"Yeah, I know," she says, the words coming in a faint whoosh. "It's just...it's not so easy."

Those words hang between us in the stillness of the room. Two red circles blotch Brachie's cheeks, and I realize that she's embarrassed.

I want to tell her that it's okay, that even near-perfect girls like her are human and entitled to their feelings — but I say nothing.

A sharp rap sounds on the door, and Ricki rushes into the room. "Sorry about that," she says. "Where are you two up to? Did you get far?"

Brachie and I look at each other and exchange slight smiles. No, we didn't get far in the script — but maybe...maybe we did get far in other ways...

"Shall we go on, Maria?" I ask Brachie, effecting a heavy Spanish accent.

"We shall," she says, pretending to snap to attention.

And then, as Ricki looks on, bemused, the two of us dissolve into giggles.

CHAPTER 22

Brachie

THIS IS THE SECOND TIME I'm bringing Atara Gold home with me. Although I'm far less nervous than the first time around, I can't help feeling somewhat anxious. As evidenced by Dassi's visit at just the wrong time last week, there are plenty of things that could go wrong.

I can't help but wonder why Atara prefers to rehearse in my house over her own. True, my house is quiet compared to hers, but her adorable sisters hardly disturbed us the last time I visited the Golds' palatial home.

"How's your mother feeling?" Atara asks somewhat hesitantly as we approach my house.

I smile wryly. If my mother weren't her principal, she wouldn't have any qualms about asking how she's feeling. I wonder if the specter of my mother's job will always haunt me, at least as long as I'm still in high school.

I decide to answer candidly. "*Baruch Hashem*, she's feeling much better."

"That's great." Atara looks uncomfortable, as if she's not sure whether she should say what's on her mind. "Do...do you think she'll be around when we get to your house?"

I look directly at her. "My mother doesn't bite, you know."

Atara looks embarrassed, and I immediately regret that last comment. I can't really blame her for feeling the way she does; anyone in her shoes would be nervous.

"She'll probably be resting," I put in apologetically, hoping for Atara's sake — not to mention mine — that my mother is safely tucked away in her bedroom, and that she'll remain there for the duration of Atara's visit. It would be so awkward for all involved if Atara bumped into my mother.

We continue the rest of the way in silence. I adjust my bulging knapsack on my back, wondering how I can have so much homework when it's only Monday. We turn onto my block — and I stop in my tracks, my eyes widening in despair.

"Is everything okay?" Atara asks me.

I nod quickly, continuing to tread onward. Except that everything is *not* okay. How can it be, when Chevy's minivan is parked right outside my house?

I grit my teeth as I let myself into the house. Despite my fervent hopes that Chevy and her brood are downstairs in the basement, they are not. I can hear loud chatter emanating from the living room — and with it, my mother's voice.

I'm about to suggest to Atara that maybe we should make a run for it and go to *her* house, when Chevy wanders into the hallway.

"Oh, hello!" she says cheerily. "I thought I heard the door open. How are you, Brachie? And who's your friend?"

"This is Atara Gold," I say stiffly. I gesture to Chevy. "And this is my sister Chevy."

"Nice to meet you," Chevy tells Atara. "I've never heard your name before."

"We're working on production together," I inform my sister through clenched lips.

Chevy smiles and looks wistful. "You know, some of my best friends from high school are the ones I made during production."

I am mortified, horrified that Chevy is sharing this with us as if…as if Atara and I are about to become lifelong friends. I want to shout at my sister, tell her off, demand that she leave the house…but right then, my mother comes into the hallway. I'm not looking at Atara — I don't *want* to look at her — but I can sense right away how she stiffens.

"Hello, Brachie. Hello, Atara," my mother greets us warmly.

"Hi," Atara says shyly.

I try to force a smile to my face, but I end up grunting instead.

Sima and Shimmy come running toward my mother. "Bubby! Bubby! Where are you? Can you read us another book?"

"I'm coming," my mother tells them calmly.

"I'm so happy to see that Sima is feeling better," I tell Chevy frigidly. "But Ima isn't supposed to be reading books. She's supposed to be *resting*."

"Actually, Ima is the one who wanted to read books to the kids," Chevy tells me, using the sugary voice that I abhor.

"It's okay," my mother cuts in. "Chevy came over to bring us some food, and I offered to read to the kids. I need a break from all that resting!" She chuckles, but I am not amused.

Chevy turns to Atara. "So, where do you live?" she asks, her tone friendly.

I glare at Chevy, the memory of our time together at the park just this past Shabbos flying out of my mind. Then, she'd been vulnerable and desperate, and I'd been quick to stretch out a helping hand. But now...

It seems like Chevy has also forgotten that hour we spent together. I glance at the toys on the floor — admittedly not as bad as the mess left by Dassi's crew — and am filled with the bitter knowledge that I'll be expected to pick up the stray pieces floating all over. From the looks of it, my sister is back to her usual demanding self.

"Sorry, Chevy," I say quickly, turning away. "We have to go. We've got a ton of homework to do tonight before we start rehearsing, and we can't waste the night talking."

I glance back at Chevy before heading up the stairs...and my heart freezes. She is staring after me, an inscrutable expression on her face.

She may drive me crazy at times, my sister — but I really hadn't meant to hurt her. Somehow, run-ins with Chevy leave me feeling like I'm all tangled up and can't figure out how to undo the knots. Everything always seems to spiral out of control so quickly.

I can't help wondering...maybe, just maybe, this time things could have been different. Or could they ever be?

I sigh heavily. Why is everything just so *complicated*?

Atara

I'VE ONLY MET TWO of Brachie's sisters, and I'm wishing I could get to know them all. They're so nice, so unpretentious...so *real*. So I'm having a hard time understanding what happened downstairs, when Brachie saw her sister. Or maybe she was just uncomfortable that her mother was there, too?

Brachie throws her knapsack onto the floor, then loses her balance and bumps into her bed. "Ouch!" she grumbles, rubbing her shin.

"Are you okay?" I ask her.

She nods but still looks upset.

"Your sister is really nice," I say hesitantly.

Now Brachie looks *really* annoyed. Oops.

"Hm-mm," she mumbles noncommittally.

"Um...maybe we should start with scene three before we tackle homework?" I venture, riffling through my own knapsack. I rummage through my books and pull out my script. I look at Brachie. She's still standing there, a faraway expression on her face.

"Uh...Brachie?"

She looks at me, but her gaze is still unfocused.

"Is...is everything okay?"

For the life of me, I can't begin to understand Brachie Bodner's odd behavior. It's like as soon as she entered her house — this warm, welcoming home — she became a completely different person.

And not a very happy one.

"Yeah," Brachie mumbles. "Everything's fine." She gives a short, hollow laugh. "Why wouldn't it be?"

I don't say anything. I am standing, waiting, wondering what could be bothering Brachie. From downstairs, I can hear the faint sounds of high-pitched laughter and childish voices jabbering happily.

I smile. "Your niece and nephew are so cute," I say, the words slipping out without me thinking. "It's so nice of your sister to bring them over to visit."

Brachie flushes, and her eyes fairly shoot sparks. "Sure, it's nice," she spits out. "And it's also nice that I'll have to pick up all the stuff they leave around, and that I'll be expected to take care of them later if my sister hangs out here any longer and —"

She stops suddenly, and her eyes widen as if she just realized whom she's speaking to. I can see the shame well up in her eyes, and I look away, trying to pretend that I haven't been listening.

An uncomfortable silence settles over the room, and when I finally summon up the courage to peek at Brachie, I'm shocked. Her eyes glisten with unshed tears.

Can it really be...that Brachie Bodner, the highly respected principal's daughter is...crying?

Brachie

I CAN'T BELIEVE this is happening.

This is the stuff dreams — nightmares, really — are made of. I'm standing in my bedroom, with its ancient furniture and walls fairly begging for a paint job, and Atara Gold is only

CURTAIN CALL • 201

three feet away from me. And I have just allowed my grievances toward my sister to tumble out of my mouth. It's all I can do to choke down the sobs.

I turn my head, pretending to busy myself with the scenery outside the window — the Kahns' house right across the street and the huge tree in our front yard, whose branches I've watched bob during many a restless night. I'm not sure if I should make a move to start reading through our lines or make some type of generic statement that glosses over what just happened. After a few moments of tense thought, I choose the latter.

"Um...sorry," I say, though I'm not really sure why I'm apologizing. "It's just...it's just hard sometimes, know what I mean?"

"Sure," Atara replies. She sounds relieved, and I'm guessing it's because I've broken the silence. "Little kids are so cute, but they can be really hard, too."

Oh, yeah? I want to say to her. *Did you ever have to do anything for your little sisters? Isn't that what live-ins are for — to make sure pampered princesses never have to lift a finger?*

I sigh, feeling bad that my thoughts are even going in that direction. Atara is a very nice girl, even if she is somewhat coddled. Is it her fault her parents have chosen a certain lifestyle?

"Your sisters are amazing," Atara says suddenly. "They're so dedicated."

"Yeah," I say flippantly. "Especially when there's a younger sister at home to be their built-in babysitter so they can relax whenever they come."

I gulp and blink, hard. Did I really just say that? What is wrong with me today?

Well, now Atara Gold knows the truth, I think bitterly. *Mrs. Bodner's daughter has her problems, after all.*

I bite my lip, hoping I didn't just reflect poorly on my mother. What must Atara be *thinking* of her, that she's raised a daughter who is such an ingrate? Of course, my sisters are wonderful people, and I really do appreciate them...most of them. For some reason, Chevy and I have tangled ever since we were little. When she got engaged, I couldn't help wishing she'd move to Eretz Yisrael after her wedding, so we'd be far, far away from each other.

But I'm not going to share that with Atara. I must rectify this situation somehow, make her think that I didn't really mean what I said and that of course, my family is just wonderful.

Wonderful, wonderful, wonderful: that's the Bodner family, in a nutshell — or at least that's the way I need other people to see us. But how to convey that to Atara? How to undo the damage my words have caused?

"I think it's nice that your sisters are so family-oriented," Atara says, almost as if to herself. "Taking care of their kids themselves, spending time with them, being there for them..."

I stare at her. Atara sounds wistful, as if she wants so badly what we Bodners have. I think of her mother, the gracious Mrs. Gold, how elegant and grand she is, and how her home is laden with every luxury in existence on Planet Earth. And with all that...could it be...is it possible...is the life Atara Gold leads not as perfect as I thought it was?

Atara looks at me and flushes. I hope my thoughts aren't

too transparent, that she can't read my mind. But there's a certain heaviness in the room as we turn our scripts to the right page. And although I try to jump into my character, to put on a pretense as the conniving Maria, I know that my lines sound subdued.

CHAPTER 23

Atara

As Brachie leads me downstairs, I find myself wondering only mildly if Mrs. Bodner will still be in the living room. Now that the awkwardness of that first encounter has passed, I am more comfortable with the notion of bumping into her in her house.

Sure enough, I can make out the sound of chatter coming from downstairs. As we pass the living room, I can see that it's empty. "They must be in the kitchen," Brachie says, answering my unasked question.

I'm somewhat relieved, but then I realize that it would only be polite to say goodbye to Mrs. Bodner. Brachie opens the front door, and I peer outside. My mother's SUV is not perched alongside the curb yet, and I give Brachie a sideways glance.

"Do you think I could say goodbye to your mother?" I ask hesitantly.

Brachie looks at me, slightly surprised, but nods. She leads the way to the kitchen. Her sister — I remember that Brachie had called her Chevy earlier — is seated at a small, round table with her children.

"Where's Ima?" Brachie asks Chevy.

Chevy looks up from spooning chicken into her kids' mouths. "She went upstairs to rest a little," Chevy says. She smoothes back her shoulder-length *sheitel*, and I study her more closely. With her black and burgundy sweater and co-ordinated burgundy skirt, she strikes me as so different from Mrs. Fleishman. Still, the resemblance between all the sisters is strong, and I'm sure that even if their temperaments are different, they must be alike in other ways.

Brachie turns to leave the room, and I give her sister a smile.

"It was nice meeting you, Atara," Chevy says. She puts a forkful of rice into her son's mouth, and he flails his small arms in protest. Suddenly, to my horror, he gives his plate a shove and it slips to the floor.

Luckily, it's only plastic, so there's no breakage, but there's quite a mess spread out over the ivory and black tiles.

Chevy sighs heavily. "I'll get to that soon," she mumbles.

Brachie reaches for the broom. "I'll take care of it," she volunteers, to my surprise.

I notice that Chevy seems just as taken aback. "Thanks, Brachie," she says softly, looking at her sister.

Brachie gazes back at her, and something — the hints of a truce? reconciliation? — hovers in the air.

The moment is broken when my mother honks loudly outside.

"I'll be back in a minute," Brachie tells her sister. She walks me to the door. "Thanks for coming," she tells me seriously.

"Thanks for having me," I reply.

We smile at each other with the shy awareness that we're thanking each other for more than just this visit. Then the moment passes, and I head quickly down the walk to my mother's car and climb inside.

Brachie

"How'd it go, Brachie?" my mother asks. She appears in the kitchen moments after Chevy and her brood leave for their own house. I can't help wondering if she was waiting for them to leave so she could eat supper in peace.

"Good, *baruch Hashem*," I say, sliding a drumstick onto a plate for my mother.

"Thank you, Brachie," my mother says appreciatively as I hand her the food. She smiles. "It's finally quiet here, hmm?"

"Yeah," I agree.

We eat in silence for a few minutes. I'm feeling rather good about myself and the way I helped Chevy out with the kids before she left — kind of how I felt on Shabbos when I held her crying baby at the park. Wonder of wonders, she didn't seem to take my assistance for granted then, or now.

Miracles do happen, I think. But as I look into my mother's twinkling eyes, I realize that it's quite possible that Chevy's metamorphosis has more to do with a motherly talk than anything else. Although I know that Chevy — and I — will lapse, at times, into the tug of war that has defined our relationship until now, I allow myself to relax for the moment...and to hope.

Supper draws to a close as I realize that it's getting late and I still haven't done any homework. I'd planned to do some assignments with Atara — but then again, nothing about this visit went as planned.

"You want some tea, Ima?" I ask as I run hot, soapy water over our few dishes.

"That would be great. Thank you, Brachie," Ima says.

I prepare some chamomile tea for my mother and then head upstairs. Once in my room, I notice a purple notebook lying on the floor, near the wall. And it's not my notebook.

I groan inwardly as I make out Atara Gold's round handwriting inside. Her notebook must have fallen out of her knapsack when she was here. I handle the notebook gingerly, not sure what to do. Should I call her and let her know I have it? Wait for tomorrow to tell her about it?

I grimace. I know that if I would've left my own notebook in someone else's house, I'd want to know about it right away. But still... I've never called Atara's house before. Girls call each other all the time, of course, and I know it's the proper thing to do right now, but when I think of the phone ringing in those big, beautiful rooms — with me on the line — I can't help but feel intimidated.

Too bad, I tell myself. I'm a big girl, and I'd better start acting like one.

I open the door to my room and head back downstairs, this time to look for a community phone book.

Atara

"How'd it go, Tari?" my mother asks as she guides the car down the dark streets.

"Good, *baruch Hashem*," I tell her. "I feel like the play is really coming together. I've already memorized most of my lines."

"Great," my mother says, but she seems distracted.

I am instantly on the alert. Anything could be on my mother's mind, really. And she *has* been in better spirits the past few days. But…

"Where are we going?" I ask as she makes a right instead of a left.

"Elisheva is playing at a friend's house," my mother says. "She went there straight after school and I haven't had a chance to pick her up yet."

"Oh," is all I say.

The car continues for a few more blocks before coming to a stop outside a modest, two-story house. My mother taps the horn, then peers at her watch.

"It's late," she says fretfully. "Daddy will be home soon, and I forgot to warm up his supper."

"He's coming home with Mr. Steinhaurt again?" The words slip out of my mouth, and my mother looks startled.

"Actually, no. Why would you think Mr. Steinhaurt is coming tonight?"

I take a deep breath. "Because he came a few times last week."

My mother doesn't say anything.

Then and there, I decide to take the plunge. To ask my

CURTAIN CALL • 209

mother, straight out, what exactly is happening in my home. "Mommy," I say. I swallow hard, then look directly at my mother. "What's going on?"

My mother shakes her head. "There's nothing going on," she tells me.

I am frustrated. There *is* something going on, and suddenly I must know what it is.

"But why did Daddy come home early those times? And why with this friend who we never heard of before? And why does everyone seem so worried lately?" The questions tumble out of my mouth faster than I can control them.

My mother is silent for a moment. Then she sighs resignedly. She opens her mouth to say something, but Elisheva chooses that moment to burst out of her friend's house and run into our car.

My mother turns around to give her a bright smile. "Hi, Shev!" she chirps. Is it my imagination, or is her perky voice tempered with relief? "Did you have a good time?"

Elisheva nods and grins. "Look what I made!"

She holds up a paper covered with heart stickers.

"How nice!" my mother tells her. She looks sideways at me and lowers her voice. "Atara…yes, I guess you could say something *was* going on… But I didn't realize that you had picked up on it and were so nervous about things. *Baruch Hashem*, everything is really all right now… I'll speak to you about it a different time, okay?" She glances meaningfully in the rearview mirror at my sister, and I nod wordlessly, wondering whether I can believe that statement that things aren't as bad as I've been imagining them to be.

The car glides smoothly down the streets. I can see lights twinkling here and there in otherwise dark houses, signs that there is life bustling behind closed curtains. I wonder if everyone's lives are as complicated as mine seems to be right now.

My mother is quiet as she concentrates on the roads. Only Elisheva keeps up a steady chatter, unaware of the tension wrapped around us like a too-tight scarf.

My mother pulls smoothly into our enormous garage, and we enter the house. Esti and Miri barrel into my mother before she even has a chance to take off her coat.

"I'm sorry, Atara," my mother tells me. "I can't speak right now. Things are a little hectic here. Let me take care of the girls first, okay?"

"Okay," I say despondently. I wonder if this talk is ever going to happen. I head to my room, for lack of anything better to do. I'm in no mood to eat supper, and I have no desire to hang around while my mother tends to my sisters.

When the phone jangles loudly on my desk, I pick it up eagerly. I could use a friend to talk to.

"Hello?" I say expectantly.

"Hi, Atara?" The voice is hesitant, as if the caller is not sure she has the right number.

"Yes?"

"It's Brachie."

"Oh!" I'm surprised — I've just come from her house, after all — but at the same time, quite pleased. "How are you?"

"*Baruch Hashem*. Um...I just wanted to let you know that you left a notebook at my house. A spiral, with a purple cover..."

I feel oddly deflated. *That's* why Brachie Bodner is calling me? "Oh," I say again, this time a trifle too flatly.

"Do you need it for tonight?" Brachie sounds concerned.

"Oh, no," I hasten to assure her. "It's fine. I'll get it back from you in school tomorrow."

"Okay, no problem."

There's a slight pause.

"So…I guess, have a good night," Brachie finally says.

I sigh heavily. "Yeah, you, too."

Another pause. Neither of us has hung up yet.

"Um…are you okay, Atara?" Brachie asks uncertainly.

I flop onto my bed and stare up at the lavender-hued ceiling. Of course I'm okay! Atara Gold is always okay! She's always wonderful, in fact. I'm trying to figure out how to express just that to Brachie, but I find myself murmuring instead a mild, "Hm-mmm."

Brachie says nothing. I'm about to say goodbye when I hear my little sisters' high-pitched voices in the hallway. Janet's even tones follow them, presumably to their bedroom. *Where is my mother?* I want to know. Has she forgotten that she agreed to tell me what's going on?

"Did you ever need to really speak to someone?" I blurt out without thinking. "And you don't know if this person really wants to talk to you?"

"I…I mean…" Brachie fumbles around for an answer, and I feel the heat rising to my cheeks. What in the world am I doing? Since when do I confide in Brachie Bodner?

With those unsettling questions comes the realization that I probably sound like I'm dealing with a recalcitrant friend — a major no-no for socially suave Atara Gold. I hurry to set that impression straight.

"I mean, it's my mother... She's really, really busy always," I say. The second the words leave my mouth, I feel my cheeks burn even more. My attempts at salvaging the situation — and my pride — have just landed me in a deeper muddle. Having a preoccupied mother is even worse than having friendship issues. Oh, my goodness. What must Brachie *think* of me?

"I can imagine," I hear Brachie say, as if from far away. "It's so amazing... She's working so hard on that auction, and it's not even like she gains any personal benefit from it—it's all purely a *chessed*. I...I really admire that."

I stare at the phone in my hand as if I've never seen it before. Did I just hear Brachie say that she *admires* my mother?! That her work on the auction is something Brachie *respects*?! I'm so shocked that I can't think of anything to say for a full minute.

"Atara? Are you there?"

"Uh...yeah, I am." I try to sound nonchalant, aware that I'm failing dismally.

"I think you should try to talk to her," Brachie tells me. "I'm sure your mother *wants* to talk to you — it's probably just that things are so hectic."

"You're right," I say. I know it's more than that — there's a specter of *something* hovering in my house that I can't understand, and that my parents are obviously reluctant to tell me about — but still, I suddenly feel lighter than I've felt in a long time. We arrange for Brachie to bring my notebook to school tomorrow — a minute detail that fails to interest me at the moment — and then I hang up the phone.

I try to view my mother through Brachie's rose-tinted lens, and suddenly I see her as an extremely special person: a wealthy woman who uses her assets and time to help other people, rather than using them just for herself. I find myself filled with newfound appreciation for my mother and the multiple projects she takes on.

I'm filled with something else, too: the desire to find my mother and have a serious conversation with her. Moments later, I'm flying down the stairs, bent on doing just that.

CHAPTER 24

Brachie

I CAN'T HELP GROANING as I flip open my science notebook in the quiet kitchen. The clock's steady ticking is the only sound in the room, other than the rustling of pages lined with notes about earth science. Ugh.

I may be considered a good student, but earth science is *not* my thing. That's why the ringing of the phone comes almost as a relief to me.

"Hello?" I say, settling the phone between my shoulder and ear. I riffle through the pages, trying to find that day's lesson.

"Hi, Brachie?"

I stiffen, instantly recognizing Chevy's voice. "Yes?" *What do you want? Weren't you just here?* I want to add. At the last minute, I clamp my mouth shut, and silently congratulate myself on my self-restraint.

"Listen," Chevy says, "I have a problem."

I wait.

"Shimmy fell, and I need someone to watch the other kids while I take him to the doctor."

I gasp. "Is he okay?"

"I think so," Chevy says. "But I just want to make sure he doesn't need stitches. I can't manage to get through to Ari..."

I hesitate. Chevy needs me. But...why me? Why can't she call any of the dozen high school girls in her neighborhood?

"I don't have time now to start making phone calls for a babysitter," she says, answering my unasked question. "The doctor is leaving soon, and I've got to get out of the house."

I sigh. I have homework, and a quiz to study for...but my sister needs help.

"How am I going to get to your house?" I ask.

"I'll have to drop the kids off by you," Chevy says. "They're already in their coats, so I'll just drive by, honk, and you'll come out and get them. Okay?"

"Wh-what?" I sputter, but it's too late. Chevy has already hung up the phone.

My mouth curls into a deep frown. How dare Chevy take the liberty of assuming that I'd be available for her! I shake my head, hard. There is no hope for this big sister of mine — no hope. She'll never change; she'll never understand that I wasn't created to be her personal, built-in nanny.

My mother walks into the kitchen. "Who was that?"

"Chevy," I say tersely. "She's taking Shimmy to the doctor, so I have to babysit for her other kids." I slam my notebook shut. There won't be any science homework for me — not right now, at least.

"What's wrong with Shimmy?" my mother asks, concerned. "They were just here…"

"He fell. Chevy thinks he might need stitches."

My mother's forehead puckers.

"Don't worry," I add quickly. "She didn't sound *that* nervous."

The bitterness is oozing from my voice, and my mother looks at me. "I know it's hard to drop everything and help her out right now," she says, "but try to remember that you're doing a *chessed* for Chevy."

"*Chessed* for Chevy," I mutter. "Sounds like the title of a book."

My mother shakes her head disapprovingly, and I flush. "Sorry," I mumble.

"Chevy needs you now," my mother says. "And I'll be here, too, to help out with the kids. But I really think that if you look at it as a *chessed*, and not as her taking advantage of you, you won't mind helping her out as much."

I am quiet. I'm not convinced that's the case — after all, Chevy's babysitting requests are not one-time things — but I'm not going to tell that to my mother.

"I'll do it," I say resignedly. It's not like I have much of a choice. Though my mother is feeling slightly stronger, I know she isn't supposed to be straining herself — which, if she'd be the one dealing with Chevy's children at this time of night, is more than likely to happen.

A car horn blares outside, and I look toward the door, then back at my mother. She smiles encouragingly at me. I try to smile back, but fail. Then I walk outside toward Chevy's minivan, hugging myself against the cold night air.

Atara

"Mommy?" I say as I careen most ungracefully into the kitchen.

My mother looks at me and holds up a finger. She is talking on her cell phone while walking up and down the gleaming floors. There is a concerned pucker on her forehead, and I'm instantly anxious.

"I see," my mother is saying. "No, we can't go ahead with it."
Go ahead with what?

"We laid out a lot of money for this," my mother continues.
So it's a money issue. My heart beats quickly as I strain to hear the rest of the conversation.

"I see," my mother says again. "You know what, I'm going to come over and take a look myself at the pieces. Maybe we can work something out."

Go where? Look at what pieces? Work something out with what?

"Mommy?" I say as she hangs up the phone. "Is...is everything okay?"

My mother sighs. "We rented matching tablecloths and runners, but the order was messed up and the company is insisting that it's our mistake, not theirs."

"You're talking about...the Chinese auction?" I'm not sure if I should laugh or cry.

My mother eyes me strangely. "Of course. What else?"

What else?! I want to say. *How about the strange things that have been going on around here? How about —*

"I'd better go on over to the Kenigsbergs'," my mother says. "They're storing a lot of the auction props in their basement, and the order was sent there. The girls are in bed already, so I'll just run out quickly before anyone misses me."

She smiles absently at me, but I can't muster up the strength to turn up my own lips. "See you soon," she says.

What about me? I want to tell her. *I may be a big girl, but maybe I'll miss you. Maybe I need you.*

My mother is already on her way out of the kitchen, leaving me behind. My eyes sting as I realize that the conversation I've been waiting for is not going to take place — at least not right now.

"Bye," I whisper into the emptiness. Then I trudge up to my bedroom, wishing I could be a little girl again and cuddle under my blankets instead of facing the mounds of homework I still have to do.

Brachie

I STARE AT THE CLOCK RESENTFULLY. I don't resent time itself, of course. It's my sister I'm upset at. I should *not* be sitting in my bedroom at 10:26 p.m., facing loads of unfinished homework. Especially when the doctor diagnosed Shimmy's cut as "nothing more than a scratch, really."

I am grateful for that, it's true…but my suspicion that my sister overreacted at my expense is flying high. Couldn't she have looked at his wound more carefully? Couldn't she have thought that maybe, just maybe, I had my own things to take care of tonight and babysitting just didn't fit into my agenda?

The phone rings somewhere in the house. It stops after two rings; it sounds like my mother has answered it. Vaguely I wonder who the caller is. I try forcing myself to concentrate on my work, but I'm *tired*. After a whole night spent distracting Sima from the fact that her mother had forsaken her, and walking up and down the halls with a cranky, crying baby, I'm ready to curl up in my own bed.

"Brachie?" my mother calls. "It's for you."

For me? I stand up and stretch, then leave my room to take the extension in the hallway.

"Hello?"

"Hi, Brachie?"

Not Chevy again! I press my lips together, tightly, knowing that I don't want my true feelings spilling out right now. Not when I'm so upset.

"I just wanted to thank you," Chevy says quickly. "You were really a lifesaver tonight."

"Hmm," I say noncommittally.

"I mean it," Chevy says, her voice heating up. "I...I know it wasn't easy for you to drop whatever you were doing and give up so much of your night for me like that. I remember all that work from high school...it's not easy."

I am quiet, touched by my sister's words. Never before has she admitted that the help she needs from me requires self-sacrifice on my part.

"I was just so nervous," she confided. "I guess blood and stitches traumatize me. Do you remember when I fell off the monkey bars years ago and needed stitches?"

I nod, then remember she can't see me. "Yes," I say, my voice low.

"Ever since then, I get frantic when I see blood," Chevy says.

"And I couldn't reach Ari. His phone was off, and I just didn't know what to do."

My heart softens. "Well, I'm glad I could be of service," I say lightly.

"Thanks, Brachie," Chevy says again. "I really mean it."

"You're welcome," I reply.

I hang up the phone and stare at it for a long time. When have I ever looked at things from Chevy's perspective — as a young mother trying to balance three small children, a house, and a job? And when has Chevy ever looked at things from my point of view — or at least let me know that she does?

I smile to myself as I pull a loose-leaf out of my knapsack. There's a first for everything, isn't there? And with that comforting thought, I try to focus on my homework.

Atara

I AM AT MY BEDROOM WINDOW the moment I see my mother's headlights illuminating the driveway.

Finally! Ignoring the piles of books on my desk — I still haven't gotten any work done — I run down the stairs.

"Hi, Mommy," I say as my mother walks into the house.

My mother smiles tiredly at me. "Hi, Atara. How'd you know I was home?"

"I was looking out the window," I say sheepishly, feeling like I'm Esti or Miri's age. "Remember you said you would talk to me?"

My mother looks confused, and my heart sinks.

"Remember?" I prod. "We were going to talk about what's going on..."

My mother's face clears. "Right. I just need to make a phone call and let Mrs. Cohen know we sorted out the tablecloth issue."

I want to stamp my foot. "Another phone call?" I say instead, my voice wobbling.

My mother looks at me. "What's the problem?"

I turn my head away. "You're always on the phone. You never talk to us...to *me*."

I know that isn't fair, but that's how I feel at the moment. Tears well up in my eyes, and I blink them away. This is so, so embarrassing.

"I'm sorry, Tari," my mother says, gazing at me with a strange expression in her eyes. "I didn't realize you felt this way."

"It's like the Chinese auction takes over our lives," I say hoarsely. "We hardly see you in the two months before the auction."

My mother looks into the distance, her expression inscrutable. Then she turns off her phone and reaches for my hand. "Come," she says. "Let's sit."

She leads me to our cavernous kitchen. I sit down as my mother putters around at the counter. A few minutes later, she brings two tall mugs and places one in front of me. Then she takes a seat across from me at the table.

"Thanks," I say. I'm not really thirsty, but a peek into the mug warms my heart. My mother has prepared my favorite drink — hot cocoa. It's been a long time — too long — since we last sat and savored hot drinks together.

There is silence as my mother and I face each over the

rectangular, glass-topped table. Janet is nowhere in sight, for once, and the background noise usually provided by my little sisters has long faded for the night.

I squirm in my seat. The setting suddenly feels a bit too formal for me. The mugs are placed strategically on dainty floral coasters, and the table beneath is shining to a polished perfection. The mood is solemn and somewhat strained.

My mind is a blank at the moment. All I can think of is my phone conversation with Brachie Bodner two hours ago. It's funny — I've always envied Brachie her mother. Not that I would want my own mother to be my principal, of course, but I'd like for her to be the type of person who *could* be...

Then I glance at my mother, and I feel some of my resentment ebbing away. The realization that she is special in her own way is one that I'm still savoring, even if I'm filled with all types of conflicting feelings. Still, the fact that neither of us is feeling too comfortable as we sit together right now is jarring.

Thankfully, my mother takes the initiative and breaks the silence. "You know, it's amazing how the years pass," she says wistfully. "It seems like just a few days ago, you were a little baby, Tari... I was so excited when you were born..."

I swallow hard as the conversation veers down memory lane. Glimpses of what once was dangle beckoningly in front of me as my mother and I begin to reminisce together. I see myself, as a little girl, sitting on my mother's lap, listening to her read a book to me...playing outside with my friends, knowing that my mother is watching me from the porch... baking cookies with my mother on rainy afternoons, sampling the cookie dough instead of forming it into neat balls while my mother looks on and laughs...

"Things are...different now," I say, trying to sound casual.

My mother glances around the sparkling, state-of-the-art kitchen. "Yes," she agrees with a sigh. "They are."

We are both silent for a moment, the faint hum of the refrigerator providing a background to our scattered thoughts.

I am transplanted back to a class with Morah Bulman from a few months ago. She was explaining the *mishnah* in *Pirkei Avos* — *Marbeh nechasim, marbeh da'agah*. Her words ring in my ears now: "The more a person has, girls, the more he worries. Let's say he has a beautiful home. He has to protect that home, doesn't he? *How* should he protect that home? With the most expensive burglar alarm? With armed guards? What about his other possessions — his fancy cars, jewelry? Girls, this person cannot stop worrying!"

I take a deep breath and return to the here and now. "Mommy," I say, "can you tell me...who is Mr. Steinhaurt?"

"Who is Mr. Steinharut?" my mother echoes. "He's actually an old friend of Daddy's, from way back when Bubby and Zeidy lived in Boro Park."

My mother doesn't seem too perturbed to deliver that explanation, and I forge on. There must be more to Mr. Steinhaurt's visits than the desire to rehash childhood memories with my father.

"So how come we never heard his name before?"

"Daddy wasn't in touch with him for years," my mother tells me. "He — Mr. Steinhaurt — is actually the one who contacted *us*, when he heard about what happened..."

"Really?" I lean forward eagerly, aware that I'm about to

crack the mystery.

My mother nods, and looks a little sad. "I'll tell you the whole story, Atara. The truth is, Daddy and I really didn't want to tell you about any of this; we didn't want to worry you. I guess we didn't count on how perceptive you are, and how worried you'd already be just by picking up on little things here and there…"

She pauses for a moment and then continues. "It all started a couple of weeks ago, when we were in Italy…"

CHAPTER 25

Brachie

LIFE IS STRANGE.

As I settle into my seat for today's assembly, I catch Atara Gold's eye and smile. I still can't believe that she opened up to me, even if just a tiny bit, on the phone last night — and that I actually gave her advice. Have stranger things happened?

I toy with the idea of asking her if she followed my suggestion — and if everything really is okay with her family at home. Perhaps under the smooth veneer of Atara's shining exterior, there are bumps and crags, invisible to the common bystander? Perhaps…perhaps *everyone's* lives are filled with their own pocks and pits, each obstacle tailor-made for each person?

I shake my head, trying to focus on Morah Bulman. She is leading today's assembly, in place of my mother. I remember my words to Atara, to speak to her own mother, and can't help repressing a grin. If there's one thing I've been doing lately, it's speaking to *my* mother — and I wonder why I never tried to do it before.

"Good morning, girls," Morah Bulman begins. She dives straight into a *devar Torah* without any preamble, so unlike my mother's calm way of building a connection with her students before launching into whatever she wants to say. Although I know my mother will be back soon, leading assemblies as always, my heart lurches. Never could I have imagined, sitting on these stiff-backed benches during school assemblies, that I'd find myself missing my mother so much.

It's strange, though. The freedom I yearned for, ever since I stepped through the doors of Bais Breindel as a timid ninth grader, is still not mine for the taking. Although my mother is not in school, and won't be back for at least another two weeks, I am still The Principal's Daughter. Girls still tiptoe around me, or at least I feel that they do, and I am ever aware of the inherent responsibility I bear to behave accordingly, as suits my status. But it's no longer the crushing burden I once felt it to be. And, wonder of wonders, I find myself, if not looking forward, then at least not dreading my mother's return to school.

I sit back, allowing my thoughts to flit to tonight's rehearsal. I smile inwardly. Production is coming together quite nicely — our play is chugging along at a rhythmic pace, with all of the actresses mastering their lines and reaching deep within themselves to unearth even more reserves of talent.

I've been an actress my whole life, it seems — and this play is just a case in point. But this play is teaching me so much more than how to perfect my acting skills; I am learning from it, unbelievably enough, how to *take off* my mask, too. Because along with the talent that is being honed under the direction of Ricki and Zehava at these rehearsals, is something even better — the chance to connect to other girls in true friendship.

And for the first time in my life, sitting among so many girls around my own age, I no longer feel so lonely.

Atara

I CAN'T HELP FEELING GUILTY. Morah Bulman is talking, her voice rising and falling animatedly, but my thoughts are still back in our kitchen, with my mother.

My mind has still not been able to wrap itself around the frightening reality my mother told me about last night: a seemingly decent businessman, one whom my father was acquainted with and trusted, who "happened" to be staying at the same hotel as my parents; a seemingly solid plan that merely served as a façade to entice innocent people to fork over chunks of money; the promise of enormous profits in just two months' time; and a post-trip visit from Mr. Steinhaurt, a well-known lawyer and my father's childhood friend, to help him figure out what to do about this mess.

I fold my arms and shiver, although the room is heated. I feel guilty again — this time about the fact that my suspicions fell on Mr. Steinhaurt, who was only trying his best to help my father. He gave of his time to meet my father at home several times, so the two could put their heads together and not only save my father, but also some other friends who were lured into giving financial backing to this "project" — a project that was never intended to get off the ground, in any sense of the word.

Talk about being *dan lekaf zechus*.

My mother refuses to tell me which of my fathers' friends were affected by this scheme — and it's best that way. She assured me countless times that my father pulled out of this "project" just in time, *baruch Hashem* — and that investigators are close on the heels of this so-called businessman, who ruthlessly planned to pull down so many while cushioning himself in the cocoon of their money.

I bite my lip, hard. The realization that the image of my family being reduced to poverty — or at least close to it — wasn't so far off, is overwhelming. And the knowledge that things we take for granted — things like our family and our financial security — are so transitory, is jarring.

A shudder passes through me, and I hug myself tightly. Yocheved, at my right, jabs me with her elbow. "You okay?" she whispers.

I nod, although I don't intend to share this escapade with her. It would be hard — too hard — to convey the anxiety I lived with this past week, the tension and worry...and the newfound closeness forged between my mother and myself last night as the minutes ticked by in our quiet kitchen.

I wonder if any of my friends could truly understand the way I'm feeling right now. And then I realize that there's one friend who surely could. I look at Brachie — the one who encouraged me to talk to my mother, thus enabling me to be feeling as wonderful as I am now. Brachie is listening avidly to Morah Bulman, but when she turns her head for a moment, I catch her eye. We both grin, somewhat shyly, before turning to face the front of the room once again.

I rest my hands on my lap, relaxing slightly. It's funny, I muse, but as self-appointed drama queen, I've been acting my whole life, putting on a pretense of perfection for all the world to see. But now — maybe for the first time ever — I know that I'm ready to stop putting on a show.

Brachie

THERE'S SOMETHING about lukewarm pizza that just reeks of rehearsals.

"Is there any more left in the box?" Rena Hoch asks, breezing into the classroom where a few of us drama members are gathered.

Atara lifts the lid of the cardboard box and peers inside. "Nope."

Rena sighs. "I'm *hungry*. Why didn't anyone save me a slice? I'm only fifteen minutes late tonight!"

I glance guiltily at a second, un-started piece on my plate and clear my throat. "Here, Rena," I say, holding out the plate in her direction. "You can have this piece."

Rena glances from me to the pizza, and then turns away. "No, thanks," she says shortly. "I don't need any favors from perfect goody-goodies." She storms out of the room just as quickly as she'd come in.

My cheeks burn, and I slowly return the plate to my lap. Atara looks at me sympathetically.

"Don't mind her," she says.

I nod, but I *do* mind. A lot. Will my every action be judged under the shadow of my mother's job?

An uncomfortable silence settles over the room, and I'm embarrassed. Perhaps the girls have forgotten — at least temporarily — that I am a Bodner, and this has been a rude reminder. Or maybe they're just feeling humiliated for me and don't know what to say. Whatever it is, I'm trying to think of a good pretext to leave the room and forget that the past three minutes ever happened.

"Just ignore her," Devora says suddenly.

I look at her.

"Things aren't easy for her," Devora says simply. "I don't think she means what she says."

I am silent, wondering if pain is what lies behind Rena's well-aimed barbs — and if perhaps I'm being too sensitive, and that's why I'm having a hard time deflecting her mean comments.

"What's —" a ninth grader starts to ask.

"Brachie isn't a goody-goody," Atara says quickly, putting down her plate.

I glance at Atara. That was quick thinking on her part — to gain control of the conversation before it can veer into *lashon hara*.

"You know," Atara says, continuing to sprout sentences, "Brachie and I rehearsed a few times at her house. Right?"

She looks at me, and I confirm her words with a nod. I'm not sure where she's going with this, and I can tell neither is she, because she smiles sheepishly at me and resumes eating her pizza.

"Was-was it weird to go there?" a petite ninth grader asks hesitantly. She looks at me. "I mean, no offense, but..."

I tense.

"Weird?" Atara repeats. "It wasn't weird at all. It was fun — lots of fun."

I allow myself to relax.

"Wasn't it, Brachie?" Atara says.

I catch her eye, and a moment later we are both laughing — really laughing. The tension rolls off me, and suddenly I am just a regular girl, eating cold pizza before play rehearsals begin for the night. I am not Brachie Bodner, Mrs. Bodner's daughter. I am simply Brachie Bodner, *me*. Because that's how I choose to think of myself right now.

"You're all invited to come visit," I tell the other girls in the room, giving them a most un-Brachie-like grin. Atara flashes me a thumbs-up, and I smile in return.

Then I snap to attention as Ricki enters the room. Rehearsals are about to start, and I'm readier than I've ever been.

Atara

I AM READY to embrace the world as I enter the school's auditorium, where play rehearsal will take place tonight. The big night is drawing ever closer, and I'm thrilled that I can slip right into my role without the added burden of worrying about my family. I've gotten pretty good at worrying lately, but I'm determined to face forward now and allow myself to get fully caught up in the magic of the play.

And magical it is. Although I've watched the same scenes

played out dozens of times, during every rehearsal I am swept into the drama of that uncertain time period of long ago, when fear and treachery were part and parcel of life.

I wait in the wings with Brachie, filled with anticipation.

"Juanita," Brachie whispers.

"Yes, Maria?" I whisper back. "Are you ready to steal the show?"

Brachie laughs. It's funny, but the sting of the roles we've been assigned has long receded. Because if there's one thing I've learned, as long as you put your heart and soul into whatever you're doing, you'll end up shining. And from the feedback we've been getting from admiring fans, I know that even though the playbill won't feature our names under the leading roles, Brachie and I are standing out in our own way.

Though I never thought I'd feel this way, that's fine with me. Especially because everything else is *baruch Hashem* fine — more than fine — with the rest of my life.

CHAPTER 26

Brachie

"Hi, Brachie?" Dassi's voice comes over the phone in a whisper.

I burst out laughing. "There's no need to whisper," I tell my sister. "Ima's not home now, and even if she was, she'd hear you on the phone if she picked up."

"That's true," Dassi admits in a regular tone of voice. I can tell that she's smiling. "Anyway, I just wanted to let you know that we're making the party at the park. It's really nice out today, and...well, it can get kind of messy when everyone's together."

I nod. Yes, I know that all too well.

"So here's the scoop," Dassi continues. "You're going to encourage Ima to take a walk with you for some fresh air."

Something occurs to me. "What if she's too tired? She's out at the doctor now, and she might be exhausted when she gets back."

Dassi is silent. "Good question."

I hope, for my sisters' sake, that this surprise birthday party will work out as planned. It was a last-minute idea, with the credit going to Chevy. My sisters have put a lot aside in the past few days to cook and bake and compile a scrapbook of family photos, all for my mother's party — and all without her knowledge of it.

When Chevy broached the idea to me just a few days earlier, I told her firmly that I could not be expected to help out — not with production looming and no letup in schoolwork. Thankfully, she hadn't pressed the issue, and things had come together pretty quickly even without my input.

But now there seems to be a glitch…

"Why don't you just do it here?" I say, surprising myself. "I can decorate the house pretty fast — we still have some balloons and streamers lying around in the basement closet. This way, if Ima is too tired, she'll just sit on the couch."

"Are you sure?" Dassi asks. "I know you're so busy…"

"Aren't you also?" I find myself saying.

"Well, I don't have homework and tests and reports and a play just around the corner," Dassi says.

"And I don't have housework and a job and children to take care of," I counter.

"Okay, then," Dassi concurs. "It'll be just a short party anyway. We don't have a program planned or anything — just some food and maybe a few speeches. I know Ima doesn't have strength for much more than that."

"Can you call everyone and tell them when to come?" I ask. I cock my head. "Actually, one minute…" I can hear the front

CURTAIN CALL • 235

door open and close as my parents come into the house. "Ima's home," I whisper urgently into the phone. "What should we do?"

"I guess see if she's going upstairs to rest," Dassi says. "If she is, you can decorate the dining room. If she isn't, maybe she'll want to go for a walk and we'll just have the party at the park."

"Okay," I agree. "I'll call you back soon."

I hang up and race downstairs.

"Hi," I say to my parents, who are seated at the kitchen table. They smile at me. "How was the appointment? How are you feeling, Ima?"

"*Baruch Hashem* to both of your questions," my mother replies, her eyes twinkling.

"Maybe you want to go for a walk now?" I ask, aiming for a casual tone.

My mother hesitates. "I don't know," she says. "I'm a little worn out..."

My father, who is in on the secret, realizes what he needs to do. "Come on, it's a nice day out," he coaxes my mother, giving me a surreptitious wink. "The sunshine will do you good. You know what? I'm home now anyway — I think I'll come also."

My mother looks a bit surprised. "Okay, if that's what everyone around here wants," she says.

"Great," I say quickly. I race upstairs and call Dassi. "Tell everyone to go to the park *now*," I tell her. "We'll be there in about fifteen minutes."

"Wonderful," Dassi says. "Thanks, Brachie!"

I hang up and run back downstairs.

My mother looks at me, amused. "Are we going for that walk or not?" she asks.

"We're going," I say sheepishly. "Sorry about that."

I throw on a jacket and walk alongside my parents, joining in their casual conversation. *When's the last time we took a walk together like this?* I wonder. I'm almost sorry when our walk comes to an end and we reach the park.

Atara

"WE'RE GOING TO THE PARK!" Miri trills. Elisheva and Esti scamper behind her, joining hands and giggling.

"We are?" I ask them.

"*We* are!" Elisheva confirms.

My mother comes up behind them, smiling. "Daddy and I are taking them to the park," she informs me. "You're welcome to join us."

I stand there, dumbfounded. When's the last time my family went together to the park…or anywhere, for that matter?

"Really?" I say.

The disbelief must have been evident in my tone, because my mother looks at me and her smile wavers. "Really."

I am instantly contrite. I hadn't meant to make my mother feel bad. "Of course I'll come," I say, and I smile as my sisters squeal in delight.

"You're not too busy with homework?" my mother asks me.

I look behind me at my desk, where books and notebooks are strewn all over. After a morning spent rehearsing, I have yet to tackle my schoolwork. But…"Some things are more important," I say.

Then I follow my sisters as they lead the way down the stairs and into the beckoning sunshine. My father joins us outside, where he has just parked his car.

I marvel that, on a regular Sunday afternoon, we are taking a leisurely stroll. Never mind that the Chinese auction is looming, or that my father's cell phone is perpetually buzzing — perhaps my talk with my mother has reaped dividends that I'd only dreamed of.

"Will you push me on the swings, Atara?" Miri asks, tugging my hand.

I look into her sweet, innocent eyes and smile. "Of course I will," I assure her.

"I want to go very high — up to the sky," she says eagerly.

"Okay," I agree. Right now I feel like I could soar up to the sky myself.

Brachie

My mother squints into the distance and looks at me, puzzled.

"Isn't that Shifra?" she asks, pointing to a tall figure walking toward a picnic bench. "And...isn't that Ettie?" Her finger moves in the direction of my sister, who is running after her son.

I freeze. "Um...maybe," I say. "Or maybe it's someone who just looks like them."

The surprise is about to be blown. I can see Chevy making her way toward Shifra, pushing a double stroller.

"Wait," my mother says. "There's Chevy." She looks at me again. "What's going on?"

I smile impishly and shrug. "Um...surprise?"

My mother starts to laugh. "That's so sweet!" she says.

"It's kind of informal," I tell her. "I mean, it's at the park..."

"I don't mind," my mother says, grinning from ear to ear. She heads over to my sisters. "What a nice idea!" she tells them.

Chevy turns to glare at me before asking my mother, "How'd you know...?"

My mother looks quickly from me to my older sister. "Well, I saw you and Shifra from a distance, and tomorrow *is* my birthday, so I put two and two together."

Chevy noticeably calms down, but I am incensed. Have I not given up a few hours of my time to escort my mother to her party? Why must Chevy have a bone to pick every time we meet?

"Sit down," Chevy tells my mother, motioning to a beach chair she's brought along. She opens a second one for my father.

"You girls always think of everything," my mother murmurs.

Chevy looks pleased. Just then I see Dassi making her way toward us, trailed by her children. Her *sheitel* is blowing in the breeze, and she looks harried.

As usual, I think peevishly. *Can't Dassi ever be on time?*

She draws closer, and I can see the disappointment on her face.

"Did I miss the surprise?" she asks. She sighs. "The baby needed a diaper change just as I was leaving, and then one of the kids' teachers called just as I was locking the door..."

She looks so sorry that I am instantly contrite. Poor Dassi.

She means well — she really does.

"I'm still surprised," my mother reassures her. She stretches out her arms and looks up at the bright blue sky. "What could be better than an afternoon spent with your nearest and dearest?"

I silently agree. And then I realize something. If I can accept Dassi with all of her faults — can't I do the same for Chevy?

I peek at Chevy, who is busy setting up cupcakes and salad on a picnic table. For all of her faults, there *is* an awful lot of goodness in her, and today, with its sunshine-y splendor, I'm determined to see it.

"I see Miri! I see Miri!" Dassi's daughter Tova suddenly squeals.

I pinch Tova's cheek and follow her gaze. My eyes widen. Hey — could it really be…?

Atara

I don't believe my eyes. Of all the people to meet in the park, it has to be Mrs. Bodner.

I shake my head quickly and try to reorder my thoughts. How would Brachie feel if she knew that's what I was thinking?

I watch Miri run off to play with Tova, Brachie's adorable niece — and Mrs. Bodner's granddaughter. I feel instantly guilty again. If *I*, who have become so friendly with Brachie recently, can't move past thinking of her as Mrs. Bodner's daughter, how should anyone else?

"Hi!" I say, flashing a big smile at Brachie. I hope it looks natural.

"Hi," Brachie answers. She looks slightly uncomfortable, but this time I don't feel slighted. Our time together has given me a glimpse of her life as the principal's daughter, and I don't blame her in the least for feeling awkward meeting me in this setting.

"What brings you to the park?" I ask.

"We're having a birthday party for my mother here," she replies.

"Nice!" I say, impressed. I watch Brachie's sisters bustling around, setting up food and paper goods.

"Aren't you Brachie's friend?" asks one of her sisters — Chevy, I recall. "I met you when you were rehearsing together."

"Right," I say.

"This is Atara Gold," Brachie reminds her. I'm surprised, and I can tell her sister is, too. The last time I'd gone to the Bodner house, Brachie seemed upset when her sister tried to make conversation with me. I'm glad that whatever was bothering her then seems to have receded.

I look at Mrs. Bodner and smile, not sure what to say. "Hi," I say. "Um…happy birthday." I want to bite back the words right away. Maybe it's inappropriate to wish my principal a happy birthday?

"Thank you," Mrs. Bodner replies, her smile warm.

I turn uncomfortably to look for my parents. They are walking slowly, Elisheva and Esti frolicking around them. Brachie follows my gaze.

"Family outing?" she murmurs.

I nod, and she catches my eye.

"That's really nice," she says, and I know she means it. "I'm so behind in homework, I could cry."

"Me, too," I say, though right now I feel far from crying.

"You'd think the teachers would have some *rachmanus* before production."

"Never," Brachie says with a grin, conveniently seeming to forget that her mother is the boss of the teachers. "Anyway, this will all be over soon — production, I mean. Then we'll get back to regular, old life. Whatever that is."

Whatever that is.

An odd ache fills me at the thought that these hours of rehearsals will soon come to an end. They've been fulfilling and fun…and, during this time, wonderful friendships have been forged, friendships that will always hold special meaning to me.

But at the same time, I realize that I'm ready to move forward. I watch Miri laughing with delight as she careens down the slide, her blonde braid bouncing behind her. I can see Elisheva and Esti, pulling my parents to the swings, and my parents smiling in turn.

I grin back at Brachie. "I'm kind of interested to find out what regular old life holds," I say.

And as the breeze ruffles my hair and the sun warms my face, I know that I mean it.

EPILOGUE

Brachie

INTERMISSION. The word is magical. It conjures up that blissful moment straddling the exhilaration of being on stage and that of accepting tumultuous congratulations from friends and family.

"Brachie!"

I have no time to wonder who is grabbing me from behind. I whirl around, my eyes glowing in a face covered in heavy stage makeup. "Dassi!" I cry, pulling my favorite sister into a bear hug. Tova, who has been allowed to come along to tonight's show with her mother, wriggles into my arms, too. I squeeze her hard.

"You were amazing!" Shifra gushes, reaching out to pull me in for a hug.

"Thanks," I say, grinning from ear to ear.

Ettie is right behind her, and I fall into her arms. "I knew you were talented," Ettie says, "but — wow!"

I am floating on the cloud of their compliments, knowing that after all these weeks of hard work, I truly deserve each and every one of them. And then I come face to face with Chevy.

My smile freezes on my face for a moment. We understand each other better these days, Chevy and I, but we still have our inevitable moments and arguments. And perhaps we always will.

"Amazing, Brachie," Chevy murmurs, looking straight into my eyes. "I'm...I'm so proud of you."

My heart melts, and the next thing I know, my sister and I are entangled in a tight hug.

"Brachie!" my mother says.

I look up to see her warm eyes smiling at me. As principal of Bais Breindel, she is being accosted nonstop during intermission by people raving about the play and her students...and about me.

A sudden wave of pride washes over me. My mother, the principal. Whoever said the two are a contradiction? I pull myself away from Chevy and allow my mother to squeeze me tightly.

"You are so talented, Brachie!" my mother whispers in my ear. I hear her loud and clear, although the noise behind stage is deafening.

"Thanks," I say shyly.

Across the room, I can spot Atara Gold, surrounded by her perfect-looking family — her mother and sisters, and an elderly woman wearing a coiffed, dirty-blonde *sheitel*, no doubt a doting grandmother. Atara looks right in my direction, and we exchange a smile of shared triumph.

We have done it. We have spent countless hours memorizing our parts, honing them to perfection. We have attended myriad rehearsals, eaten cold suppers, and given up lazy Sunday mornings — all for the sake of the play. And we have connected in a way that we never could have done without the play to bring us together.

My eyes mist over suddenly, amid all the commotion and camaraderie. I am surrounded by family and friends, and I feel fuller than I've ever felt before.

"Intermission is only for another seven minutes," Ettie notes, looking at her watch.

A surge of excitement rushes through me. If the first half of the play was spectacular, the second half will be even better! And suddenly I can't wait to get back onstage.

Atara

"I'M SO NERVOUS, I'm so nervous," I chant in a whisper.

Brachie laughingly shushes me as we wait in the wings, but I know that she's just as nervous as me.

Been there, done that, I tell myself. We've already been through the first half of the play. We've already waited in the wings in anxious anticipation, hearts thudding wildly and fists clenched tightly as we bided the time until our dramatic entrance on stage. So, we should be old hands at this already — except that the exhilarating feeling which precedes any entrance onstage can never grow stale.

I can hear Nechama Korn wail loudly, bemoaning her

"parents'" capture by the Inquisition. Brachie and I glance at each other, terror in our eyes. That's our cue.

We inch forward, two cunning servants intent on destroying some more lives. And then we're there, on center stage — staring into the bright lights, hundreds of pairs of eyes focused on us. Somewhere out there are my family, my teachers, my neighbors, and many, many other people, lots of whom I don't even know. They came here tonight to be captivated by our performance — and we're poised on the brink of giving them that experience.

"Juanita!" Brachie hisses, waving a broom in my direction. Her voice echoes around the auditorium.

I nod as I furiously brandish a *shmatte* and attempt to polish an antique-looking candelabra to gleaming perfection. For a crazy moment, I want to laugh aloud as I think of Janet bringing my own house to its shining glory.

"The girls," Brachie says pointedly. She motions to Gracia and Francesca, standing frozen at the side of the stage.

My heart beats wildly. For a moment, the line I am supposed to say in response dangles tantalizing in front of my eyes, barely within grasp. My mind is blank, empty, and I start to panic. I glance anxiously at Brachie, and she looks calmly at me, willing me to come up with the right line.

And I do. "What about them, Maria?" I hear myself say, to my immense relief.

"They're next," Brachie says, her ominous voice accompanied by equally portentous background music.

We glide through the scene, and then finally — an eternity later, or maybe it was only a few minutes? — make our escape to backstage.

"Phew!" Brachie breathes, dropping her duster on the floor.

"Tell me about it," I agree. I adjust my frilly white cap and wink at her.

"Only two more scenes to go," Brachie says, somewhat nostalgically.

"C'mon, it's not over yet," I tell Brachie. "We still have another two performances after this."

Brachie brightens at that. Following this Motza'ei Shabbos show, we will be performing again on both Sunday afternoon and Sunday night. It's a whirlwind weekend, filled with heightened emotions and lots of anxiety — and I'm cherishing every moment of it.

The rest of the play passes in a hectic blur, until the triumphant finale. As the names of the cast are being called, and each actress comes onstage to be introduced to the audience, Brachie and I wait in the wings, both of us wearing identical, face-splitting grins.

Then we hear our names, as a twelfth grader announces loudly into a microphone, "Maria...Brachie Bodner! Juanita...Atara Gold!" To deafening applause, we step out into the limelight and wave to the audience. Then we move back to join the rest of the cast, waiting for the other starring actresses to be called in.

Brachie and I link arms as we join in with the finale's chorus. Around us, girls press closely together, singing in harmony. Right now, we're all in harmony, reveling in the success of our performance.

"Curtain call!" someone calls out.

Brachie and I laugh as we join our friends in taking mock bows. The curtain will soon fall on this performance. Props will be packed away; costumes will be laundered and folded neatly until they're needed again. The beautiful scenery will be rolled up and placed into storage, and soon, all we'll have left of this play will be warm memories and glossy photos.

But, as I link hands with my friends and we start to dance, I know that the curtain will never fully drop. It will only continue to rise, slowly and magnificently, over the rest of our lives.